THE DEAD END OF DYING

Bill Jack

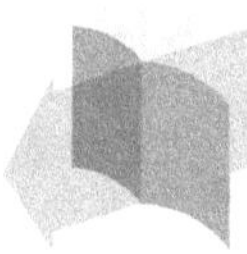

Chapbook Press

Chapbook Press
Schuler Books
2660 28th Street SE
Grand Rapids, MI 49512
(616) 942-7330
www.schulerbooks.com

Printed at Schuler Books in Grand Rapids, MI on the Espresso Book Machine®

Library of Congress Control Number: 2012955552

ISBN 13: 9781936243433
ISBN 10: 1936243431

© Bill Jack, 2012

Cover Art by Rebecca Sitterly

CHAPTER ONE
GARCIA'S

Garcia's on Central. An April Saturday morning with not a cloud in the sky, temperatures to reach the 70s, the Farmer's Market to get to, and the rest of the day for each other. A promise for at least part of the afternoon going from the hot tub at the town house in Old Town to bed and back. Alexandra Kennedy and Wilson Bennett were in their favorite booth with their favorite waitress awaiting the huevos rancheros and sopaipillas they loved. Albuquerque in the spring and time on their hands.

They held hands waiting for the food and talking over the events of the world, bemoaning the state of the universe as was their Saturday morning custom. Married for just over three years, Alex and Will were still on their honeymoon. Will had moved to Albuquerque from the Midwest, had initially joined one of the big defense firms and then two months ago, along with four colleagues, had struck out on his own. More work, so far less money but clients out the wazoo, payments being made on time, and a working environment he loved. Elizabeth LaRue, his assistant who had followed him from Michigan, was with him as well.

Alex, long a plaintiffs' trial lawyer with a national reputation, had been appointed by the Governor six years ago to the district court bench. Once a firebrand of an advocate, Judge Kennedy had quickly learned the importance of evenhandedness and a judicial temperament and had easily earned the respect of even those who had once waged war against her.

A rare day off for Will and a leisurely start to what promised to be a beautiful day. Until his cell phone rang. Ordinarily he would let it ring itself to voice mail, but he checked and saw it was his partner, Morton Blackwell. With an apologetic look to Alex, he slid out of the booth and walked outside as he answered.

"Morton? This better be good. Huevos on the way."

Quiet for just a moment. "Will, Ron's dead. Shot himself at his desk probably last night. Found him this morning at 7:30 when I came in. Place is crawling with cops, EMTs, Medical Examiner, everybody. I need you down here right now. Right now." Blackwell as always to the point, measured, calm but only just.

Stunned and unable to breathe, Will stood on the sidewalk and let it sink in. Morton Blackwell on the line telling him their new partner, Ron Johnston, had killed himself. Ron, serious to a fault, a stickler for details like no other, and a major rainmaker for the real estate business in greater Albuquerque. One of Bennett's closest colleagues. Honest as the day is long. Dead. Suicide. Gunshot. What the hell?

"I'm on my way, Ron. Have you called Ellen and Luis?"

"Not yet. They're next. Get here, Will." Blackwell's voice now beginning to tremble. Will hung up and walked back in. Alex had just taken her first bite of the green chile eggs when she looked up and saw Will's expression. She knew him far too well and knew something was terribly, terribly wrong.

"Will?"

He finally took a breath. "Ron killed himself at the office. I have to go."

Alex, without missing a beat, put her fork down, turned around to look for Barbara to get the bill, and quietly said, "Will, *we* have to go." Barbara, also sensing the urgency, hurried over to the booth with the bill. Alex threw the money on the table and they were out the door, walking quickly to the car, questions swirling unspoken between them. Questions that would take months to answer.

CHAPTER TWO
THE OFFICE

They raced down Central towards the business district and the rehabbed building that housed the law firm of Johnston & Blackwell, PA. Alex driving and Will mindlessly rubbing his hands on his thighs telling her word for word what Blackwell had told him. Trying to get his mind around what had happened. There was little to be said because neither knew anything other than what Will had been told.

As they approached 5th and Central, they were stopped behind several cars. Ahead, Central had been cordoned off with police cruisers blocking the road. Beyond, Alex and Will could see emergency vehicles, police officers on the sidewalk and yellow police tape across the front of the Lewis Building. Alex spotted a Loading Only spot a half block east of 5th, made an executive decision, and eased into it. Nobody would be loading anything with this going on down the street.

They walked quickly to the corner and were stopped by a uniformed officer clearly enjoying his time in the limelight of a major crime event. Kennedy flashed her judicial badge, which should have meant nothing to the young officer but obviously did, and he let them pass down the street. At the front of the building, another officer stood guard and was less inclined to be impressed. He looked at Kennedy's badge and Bennett's business card and radioed upstairs to the offices of Johnston & Blackwell.

Within two minutes an Albuquerque detective walked out and greeted them. Kennedy knew her from the times that she had testified in her court. Margaret Espinoza was an Irish Hispanic veteran of the ABQ Police Department and was homegrown. Years as a patrol officer, sitting for the detective tests, passing with flying colors, and for the past several years slowly pushing the glass ceiling of gender upward despite her superiors' efforts to the contrary. Kennedy took comfort in seeing her.

Bennett introduced himself to the detective and asked to be allowed upstairs. As they were talking, Ellen Phillips arrived, breathless and nervous. She was a striking woman of forty five, herself a veteran of law firm glass ceilings and now generally recognized as one of the best health law lawyers in the state. Tall, fashionable, dark hair, in great shape from daily exercise, she was normally the picture of calm. Not this morning. She hugged Will, "True? Dead? What happened!?!"

Will held her for a minute and then eased back. Espinoza gave the OK to the uniformed officer and led Kennedy, Bennett and Phillips inside to the elevator.

The Lewis Building, built in the late 1800s, had survived dozens of owners and tenants over the years. Her brick front and foundation had withstood the tests of time and she continued to be a part of the Central Ave/Route 66 history of Albuquerque. The first floor was dedicated to retail, the next two floors to office space, and the fourth floor to storage and pigeon nesting. Johnston & Blackwell took up one half of the second floor. The firm had taken over an existing lease from a plaintiffs' firm whose line of credit with Wells Fargo and lack of good cases to pay it off had finally done them in. Lavishly decorated with Southwestern art and furniture, Wells Fargo had allowed the new firm to occupy the space on practically a turn key basis.

The foursome got off the elevator, added only a few years before to accommodate the ADA laws, walked down the hallway and entered the offices of the law firm. The reception area was filled with various law enforcement and EMT types. Detective Espinoza led them through the crowd to the main conference room down the central hallway. Further down, Bennett could see the door to Ron's office on the right, the ubiquitous yellow tape across the open door, and medical types and photographers in and out of the office. His own office was the next door down.

They entered the conference room and saw Morton Blackwell seated at the head of the table. With him were two additional detectives who introduced themselves as Detective Anderson and Detective Mendez.

Before anybody could talk, Luis Moreno was escorted to the conference room by another uniformed officer. Taciturn and not wont to share his emotions with anybody but his closest friends, Luis was clearly undone by the news of his partner's death. His usual "every hair and pleat in place" was missing and, but for the fact he was wearing jeans and a Lobos T-shirt instead of pajamas, Will was sure the call from Blackwell had woken him from a Saturday morning sleep in. His eyes were red rimmed and his body was in constant motion even when he sat down in one of the leather chairs.

The four remaining principals of Johnston & Blackwell were now present, along with Judge Kennedy with a death grip on her husband's hand under the table. With coffee poured, Detective Anderson, junior in age, led off. Bennett quickly came to the unsubstantiated conclusion that the florid face and too many donuts on his young frame belied a cruelty and smug satisfaction about giving tragic news to a group he hated: lawyers. Will took a breath to hold his emotions.

"Mr. Blackwell called 911 at," a pause to look at his notebook, "7:46 AM reporting that there had been a death at the Lewis Building. Officers and EMTs were dispatched and arrived at...," another pause, "8:02. Mr. Blackwell was waiting downstairs and escorted the officers to Mr. Johnston's office. Officers found the victim at his desk, apparent gunshot wound to the right temple, blood and apparent brain matter on the left side of the desk. Vital signs checked and no response." Kennedy rolled her eyes, 'you think?'

"Head on the desk, arms outstretched, .45 caliber hand gun on the desk. EMTs confirmed the lack of vital signs, crime scene was secured, and Homicide and the ME's office were called."

Clearly a big speech for Detective Anderson, silence in the conference room as each absorbed the dispassionate recitation of a life forever gone.

"Why Homicide?" Phillips asked.

"Any death caused by gunshot goes to Homicide," said Mendez. "When we arrived, we took a statement from Mr. Blackwell who indicated that he arrived at the office around 7:20 to 7:30, didn't realize anything was wrong, stopped to make a pot of coffee in the kitchen, walked down the hall, looked in Mr. Johnston's office, and then called 911."

"I didn't touch anything," Blackwell said in what Bennett would best construe as a squeak. He wondered a moment why he said it but then left it for later. Emotions too raw and fresh, people can say anything.

"We are running the gun for..." Mendez started and Luis Moreno stopped him.

"Ron had a .45 caliber gun, kept it in the bottom drawer of his desk. He'd had it for a few years, took some lessons when he got it, and then said he kept it around 'just to be safe.' Maybe it's the same one."

"Thank you, Mr. Moreno. We'll start there. Mr. Johnston's computer was on and there was a message he had written that one would describe as a suicide note. Addressed to Judy?" And Mendez looked for information.

Kennedy had long thought that lawyers, who ought to know better than anybody, had the loosest lips of any collective group she knew and this meeting was Exhibit A.
This time it was her own husband.

"Judy is his wife. They were separated for a few weeks. Still trying to work things out."

"We want to go over the note and the computer before we reach any conclusions." The detective stopped as they heard the wheels of a gurney make its way down the hallway. Everybody turned to see it go by with a black body bag containing what had once been Ronald Johnston, Esq. Almost a moment of silence, but not quite.

"We'll need statements from each of you on your relationship with Mr. Johnston, how long you've known him, whether he was depressed, anything that might help, but we can do that later." Now Detective Espinoza taking over the mop up operation. "We know you've been through a lot. We'll have to keep the office closed for at least today and probably tomorrow but we'll let you know when we're done. Anything you need from your own offices, please get it now." Only Ellen Phillips said she needed a couple of things to work on at home, left for a moment, and returned with a brief case.

Detective Espinoza stood up to escort them out of the building. She walked next to Kennedy and as they left the building, said quietly to her. "I'm sorry, Your Honor." "Thank you, Detective." The detective gave the judge's arm a soft squeeze and left to go back up to the offices.

The five of them stood outside the building for a moment at a loss over what had happened. Finally it was Alex who suggested that the four of them go someplace for a cup of coffee and sort out the next steps. She kissed Will, told him she'd see him at home, and walked to the car.

CHAPTER THREE
HISTORY

They settled on the restaurant at the Hilton, walked themselves there and collected in a booth.

On the way over, Will, in step with Luis Moreno, thought about the last years and months they had known each other. Will himself, with the insurance defense firm, had tried four serious cases in the first year and a half and had won them all but at a great price of too many hours on too old of a body.

One of the lawyers he had battled was Luis, a native of Albuquerque, and one of a few very good plaintiffs' attorneys in the area. Several months after the trial, Luis had called out of the blue, asked Will for a drink, and had proposed that they join forces. Luis had more work than he knew what to do with, had done his due diligence on Will, and had liked what he had seen. Will, truly flattered, wanted to chew on it, and they parted with Will to get back to Luis. Alex had presided over some of Moreno's cases and couldn't have been more supportive. It wasn't like they were desperate for his paycheck, and although Will was a tad old to be starting over, she thought it well worth it.

While Will was doing his own due diligence on Luis, Morton Blackwell had approached him about starting their own firm. Morton was a young partner in Bennett's firm with a very large book of corporate business work. It didn't hurt that his father-in-law was the former mayor of Albuquerque and long touted as a potential governor or US Senator. Morton was chafing at what he felt were the inequities of being a young partner not being given his due, and was encouraged by his father-in-law to start his own shop. He needed a litigator to support the business practice and chose Will in part because he wouldn't be around forever, and in part because of the reputation Will had earned in a very short period of time.

Will told him about his talks with Moreno and vice versa, and both Blackwell and Moreno thought it could do wonders for all three of them.

One more thunderbolt happened when, serendipitously, Blackwell was approached by Ron Johnston and Ellen Phillips. They had a small practice together that had specialized in real estate and health law but were struggling with how to grow the firm against the competition of the larger firms. Blackwell called a meeting and cards were put on the table. At the end of that Monday night meeting, the five agreed to take the rest of the week to mull it over.

Will relied heavily on his wife for advice especially because he was on her turf. They had become the very best of friends after a long distance relationship that would have taxed the very best of lovers. They were that from the beginning. They also saw something in each other that kept them coming back over and over, until worn out by the exhaustion of too much time apart, they thought it best to make a decision and let the chips fall. The timing was good. Will's daughter had started college, many of his colleagues from his firm in Michigan were retiring or doing something else, his parents were both gone, and Michigan winters weren't getting any better. So he wrapped things up in Michigan but for the lake house that he would hold on to forever and moved to Albuquerque.

Alexandra Kennedy was still striking at age 55, able to turn young men's heads and proud of it, and just as sexy to Will as she had ever been. Will Bennett, just a few pounds past his prime even with biking and skiing, but with more energy at 57 than most men half his age, was finally with the love of his life. Most of the time. The two of them had a marriage counselor on retainer to remind them sometimes that they still loved each other. The nuclear winters that used to drive them and their cheerleaders crazy were now far more infrequent than the courting days, when all it took was for one of them to get on an airplane and get the hell out of wherever the winter had occurred. Only to return again and again and again.

And so the week of reflection went by and Kennedy and Bennett talked pros and cons. The biggest con was that Will would be the one bringing the least amount of business to the new venture because all of his work came from the firm. She loved Moreno and really wanted Will to work on the plaintiff's side of the bar; she knew of Blackwell and thought he had married well but also knew him to be a talent in his own right. Johnston and Phillips she knew not at all but thought their practice could do nothing but help keep the boat afloat while everybody else was gearing up.

And so came that fateful Friday. Will emailed the four and told them he was in. Within an hour, affirmatives came from all four and the group met at Ellen Phillips' condo in the Heights to plan the future. It went surprisingly well logistically. Ron Johnston had found the space in the Lewis Building through his real estate contacts and it was standing empty; Moreno's lease was up in two months from space he hated anyway, and Blackwell and Bennett could simply walk. The foursome decided on Johnston & Blackwell for the name of the firm to take advantage of their reputations and name recognition. They all had too much to drink and Ellen Phillips was particularly effusive in talking about the future. Her hug as Will was leaving lasted longer than it should have and Will had a momentary hiccup wondering what that was all about. He put it off to the excitement of the evening and the alcohol consumed. He shouldn't have.

Over the weekend, Will spoke with Liz LaRue to make certain she would come with him. The answer was never in doubt. They had been together for too long and had been through the best and worst of the journey to let a little thing like dislocating to New Mexico where she didn't know a soul to starting with a firm where she knew nobody, to now being told there was a new chapter where paydays might be a little tight for awhile.

The announcement Monday to the firm was a story that didn't begin well and ended very badly for everybody. Blackwell and Bennett were given the week to clean things up and were forbidden to contact any clients. For Bennett it was a relief, but for Blackwell it was a little more of a pragmatic problem. He solved it by calling his father-in-law who called the most important clients, got their assurance they would follow Morton, and that was that. It was hardly a happy good bye come Friday and a relief to be out of the office. Liz and Will met for a drink at the Coppertop to celebrate, were joined by Alex, and then Morton and his wife, Socorro. Ginny Michaels, Morton's assistant who was also coming with the group, was there as well. She and Liz had gotten on well at the firm and were as excited as anybody about the new venture.

Kennedy immediately took to Socorro who was a stay at home mom with two small kids but with lots of charity and community connections. She had both a personal warmth about her and an understanding of who she was in the city given her heritage. She seemed comfortable both in the role of young mother and community leader. Kennedy always had to be careful given her position on the bench, but she hoped the new firm would bring new friends to her and Will.

On Saturday, Blackwell and Bennett, with Liz and Ginny helping, moved into the new digs. The prior tenants had not been shy about either office size or lavish accoutrements. In all of his years, Bennett had never had an office as large or luxurious. Never one for trappings, he allowed himself the selfish notion that he deserved it after all the years toiling in the vineyards of the civil justice system, and then quickly put the notion away before anybody could sense it about him. On the desk left over from prior tenants were several files from Luis Moreno and three from Ron Johnston, all either already in litigation or soon to be. Johnston & Blackwell, PA was in business and life was good. Morton had put together the necessary documents that included the partnership agreement, they had purchased the necessary business, health, key man, worker's compensation, and liability insurance through the Sullivan Insurance Agency and they were in business.

That night Alex and Will celebrated.

The next two months were the happiest of Will's professional career. Until the April Saturday morning phone call changed it all.

CHAPTER FOUR
REQUIEM

In the booth the four of them ordered coffee, and stared at each other trying to let reality sink in. Of the four, Ellen Phillips was now the most composed, and Will found that a bit odd simply because she had known Johnston the longest. Blackwell quietly crying, Moreno "mi Dios" over and over, his eyes darting from one to the other, and Will sitting absolutely motionless.

Ellen's first words broke the reverie. "What do we tell his clients?"

Will thought to himself that, of all the things she could have said, 'What do we tell his clients?' was the weirdest. Apparently, Moreno thought so as well.

"'What do we tell his clients?'" Moreno said incredulously. "A man you worked side by side with for 12 years blows his brains out in his office and you want to talk about how we announce it to the world? What are you thinking, Ellen?"

She seemed taken aback but only momentarily. "He's dead, Luis. Nothing we get to change about that. He's got a thousand irons in the fire, clients we know nothing about, it will be the live story all afternoon and tomorrow. People are going to be calling all of us and the switchboard will be going crazy Monday. We need to have a plan. What is it?"

Maybe thinking about something else other than what Morton had seen that morning and what they all were feeling was what they needed to do first and let the grieving come after. There would be plenty of time for that.

The politician in Blackwell took over. "We need to work on a press release right away and get it out before we leave here, then we need to get his client list and begin making phone calls. Ellen, you and I ought to do that because we know them best. We'll need Beverly's help to pull the list together."

Will interrupted him. "We have to tell her." Beverly Davis had been Johnston's legal assistant for eight years. There had been rumors about the two of them since the firm opened and, according to Liz, before that. Elizabeth had told Will that the odds in the office were that the relationship between Beverly and Johnston had been what caused his separation. Will's initial reaction was that this was going to get a lot worse before it got better.

He volunteered to call her as soon as they were done, assuming it would take a while for the news to hit the streets. He was wrong. Just as he got the words out of his mouth, his cell phone rang. It was Alex telling him that the TV stations were breaking into their regular programming to announce the probable suicide of a prominent Albuquerque lawyer. He hung up, announced the information to the group, and told Blackwell to put the press release together while he called Beverly Davis. He left the booth, found her cell phone number in his contacts list, got her voice mail and left a message that she should call him as soon as she got the message.

When he got back to the booth, the flesh was on the release and Morton was on the phone to his father-in-law to get the former mayor's PR firm on board. Ellen Phillips was making notes on a paper napkin with Moreno studying her across the booth.

It occurred to Will that they had to tell the rest of the staff as soon as possible hopefully before they heard it via TV or press. He and Luis split up the numbers they had for the staff and decided to call a meeting that afternoon of everybody they could get hold of. They left Ellen in the booth by herself busy making notes.

CHAPTER FIVE
COMING TOGETHER

At 3:00 PM sharp, Morton Blackwell called the meeting of the full firm together in the living room of Alex and Will's townhouse in Old Town. By the time they had all arrived, each had been told by Will or Luis what had happened and each had seen it on TV. "PROMINENT LAWYER COMMITS SUICIDE" was the lead with speculation by some of those interviewed that domestic trouble may have been the cause. So much for "privacy", Alex thought to herself.

Will looked around the room. In addition to Will, Alex, Morton Blackwell, Ellen Phillips and Luis Moreno, the group consisted of Elizabeth LaRue, Debra Ramirez, Ellen's assistant, Rebecca Jackson, Luis' assistant, Ginny Michaels, Morton's assistant, Jackie LaPointe, the self proclaimed "gofer" and IT expert of the firm, and Jamee Dawe, the office manager who had been in the same position in Will's old firm.

The only person they hadn't been able to reach was Beverly Davis.

Ellen Phillips had asked Morton Blackwell to call Judy Johnston to express all of their sympathies, again a request that Will found incongruous and surprising. He had spoken to Judy's sister and left the message.

Blackwell started the meeting by talking about how devastated he was and how badly he felt for all of the people who knew Ron. It was still way too early to know anything about the "arrangements" and they would be a little difficult given the domestic distranquility between Ron and his spouse. He talked about the need to pull together, find strength with each other, and some other stuff Will and Alex both tuned out. Alex looked around the room.

Elizabeth was composed and had her game face on, Debra Ramirez and Robin Washington were holding each other and crying quietly, Ginny Michaels was teary eyed but holding it together, and Jamee Dawe could not be read at all. Jackie LaPointe, most recently a computer geek with the Alexandria, Virginia Police Department, clearly would have preferred a computer screen to the emotional baggage in the room. Moreno and Phillips by now were over the worst of the initial shock.

Morton's talk came to an end and brought Will back to the group.

Each person was given the opportunity to speak whatever was on their mind. Several spoke of Ron Johnston's work ethic, his commitment to his clients, his commitment to the profession. No one really spoke of who he was as a person and Alex thought that sadly odd. Ellen Phillips' only comment was that "We'll all miss him." Will hoped somebody would do better for Ron at his memorial service. Maybe a minister who didn't know him? He wondered vaguely if Ron even belonged to a church and was struck by how little anybody knew him.

They next talked about what to say to clients and people in the community, and the consensus was the less said the better with Morton Blackwell and/or his father-in-law's PR firm to be the "official" spokespeople. Next on the agenda was how to handle Ron's clients. While they were technically clients of the firm, Johnston & Blackwell, PA was still in its infancy and there was little, as in no, expertise in the real estate arena that could give the kind of legal representation equal to the clients' needs. The lawyers at the meeting made a short list of attorneys in Albuquerque who could do the work and assignments were made to call them first thing Monday to get their approval to give out their names as substitutes for Ron Johnston. Special preference would be given to those lawyers who understood quid pro quo.

Jamee Dawe indicated she would get with Beverly Davis first thing Monday to co-ordinate pulling the files together and to make sure bills went out to the right people.

Without Davis being there, little more could be done about the near future. Alex invited the group to stay for drinks and snacks but the only ones who stayed were Luis Moreno, Elizabeth LaRue, Jamee Dawe and Jackie LaPointe. Everybody else seemed to have some urgent place to go, as in anyplace but here, Will thought.

CHAPTER SIX
BREAKING BREAD

As Will took drink orders, he had the opportunity to reflect on those gathered in the living room. Luis Moreno was a living legend in New Mexico who had made a remarkable amount of money representing injured people, and who had given away almost as much as he made supporting local Hispanic boys and girls clubs. An unwanted orphan for the first six years of his life, he had never forgotten the desolation of loneliness and did as much as he could with his money and his time to guarantee other kids had a better start than he. Liz was one of Will's best friends and was as loyal to him as he was to her. They had been through all the joys and tragedies life brings at you and had stood side by side through it all. She was now seriously involved with a much younger man and soaking up every minute of life in love.

Jamee Dawe was a striking African American who stood 6' tall in her socks and had a model's figure and a computer-like brain. Born and raised in Harlem, her parents had gotten her the best education they could afford on the three jobs they held between them. On a basketball scholarship to Rutgers, she had played on two Final Four teams before graduating with honors. A short failed attempt at professional basketball and she found herself in a not very satisfying accounting job married to a physically abusive alcoholic. Pregnant and scared to death of her husband, she up and left Brooklyn one night and headed west. She landed in Albuquerque five years ago with the clothes in her car, a few dollars in cash, and nothing else. She got herself an apartment, wrote her husband to get a divorce, and never told him about her daughter born eight months after she arrived. Up to the time of Nakayla's birth, Jamee Dawe worked for various temp agencies doing anything from clerical to accounting. One of her last stops was at Will's firm as a fill-in assistant office manager. By the time she was ready to return full time, the firm needed an office manager and she interviewed and was hired.

There had been some talk according to Liz that Dawe had been involved with one of the senior women partners but both she and Will had been through enough of that in Michigan and left the rumor mills to the others. All they knew was that the office operated with great efficiency and that Jamee was extremely popular with the staff. All of that made it all the more surprising that the Monday after Will and Morton had announced they were leaving, Jamee had asked if there was room for her to manage the firm. A quick consult with the others and Jamee was hired. Will asked her one time why she had decided to leave and he had gotten such a non answer in response that he dropped it. After a glass of wine with Liz, she had confided in her that the atmosphere at the old firm was a little too white and a little too oppressive, the latter view of which Liz wholeheartedly supported. Since the new firm had started Jamee had been the glue, making certain the new partners and staff worked as well as they could together, making certain bills were going out, and making certain the payroll was always on time. She rarely mentioned her social life other than her time with Nakayla. Both Will and Alex thought being black in Albuquerque couldn't be easy even for as beautiful a woman as Jamee.

And then there was Jackie LaPointe. Will had first met her when she was with the Alexandria Police Department as a techie. She had "wired" him for a meeting with his best friend's wife's lover after the wife had been killed. She was tattooed and pierced and generally anti-social but Will had liked her, albeit at the same time thanking the angels that his daughter Grace had gotten all the way through law school with only a yellow rose tattoo on her wrist. Jackie had sent him cards and notes in the hospital after he had been shot, and after he had returned to Albuquerque, had kept in touch via email and an occasional text message. She had arranged a visit to Albuquerque for the balloon festival the preceding October and had stayed with Alex and Will at the townhouse. Behind the tattoos and piercings was a brilliant and inquisitive mind, and her computer talents notwithstanding, both of them were impressed with the depth of her knowledge about the world and the passion she brought to the causes she believed in.

When the new firm was being put together, Will broached the subject of having an IT person on site. The rest weren't sure that they would need somebody full time but agreed having somebody there to make the trains run on time made some sense. Jackie, back in Virginia, was offered a part-time position she grabbed at. She had packed and moved cross country in her Jeep Wrangler that she called "Rusty" for obvious reasons with a bumper sticker across the top of the windshield that read upside down, "If You Can Read This, Turn Me Over". She stayed at the Kennedy and Bennett abode while she found a place of her own, and immediately endeared herself into a full-time job doing everything from fixing computers to getting coffee to couriering documents to the court on a minute's notice. She became the firm favorite and seemed to blossom in the desert. Rumor had it there was a love interest, but questions about it were met with a blushed silence.

Will Bennett looked at them all, met Alex's eyes, and knew even with the tragedy of Johnston's suicide, he was in a very good place.

It took the second round of drinks and some good eats for tongues to loosen up. Always a short ball but happy hitter, Liz LaRue wondered out loud where Beverly Davis was. That started a conversation between Liz and Jackie and Luis on what apparently was an almost out in the open relationship between Davis and Johnston. To their understanding, they had been together for a number of years, he had stayed with his wife, Judy, for the kids' sake, and he was going to leave her when the kids got older. Alex and Will did a simultaneous eye roll having heard that story a dozen times or more. Something had happened some weeks ago when Beverly let it be known to the staff that Johnston had moved out of the house and was staying temporarily with friends until "we find our own place." Johnston's kids were still young and there was some discussion around the coffee maker as to what had happened to speed up the process.

Over the next several days, it had appeared to the staff that Ron Johnston was tired and isolated, an observation that had completely missed Will. He spent most of the time in his office with the door closed although there were blocks of time that

Beverly was with him. Still too early in the firm's history to know what it all meant, it was tolerated but duly noted by apparently everybody but Will. Jamee Dawe, quiet through most of the early vetting, offered that another unnamed staff member had raised the issue with her just the past Wednesday, suggesting that the relationship was becoming a distraction for everybody. Except for Will. And that Jamee was coming closer to having to have a sit down with both Johnston and Davis, a meeting she didn't savor and now a meeting she would never have to have.

Luis said he had spoken with Johnston about the separation and had gotten a completely different story. Yes, Ron had been involved with Beverly, and yes, it was causing problems in the marriage. (You think? Alex thought to herself.) But Johnston was clear that he wanted to save the marriage and that he and Judy were in "serious" marriage counseling (is there funny marriage counseling? Alex wondered having been through her share of the "serious" kind) and that he hoped and prayed it would all work out. What was left unsaid was what was going on at the moment with Beverly Davis.

They all talked about the finality of suicide even in the depths of marital discord, and each of the living sat around the room concluding that as bad as it was, suicide with a couple of young kids who needed a dad seemed a bit extreme. The group collectively wondered if there were something else going on. Nobody had an answer.

The survivors stayed longer than Will and Alex had bargained for, but fortunately they all decided to leave as the last of the jug of Chardonnay was consumed. Jackie was last at the door, gave both Alex and Will hugs, and then stopped for a moment.

"It isn't quite right. You know that, don't you? It isn't quite right." And then she was out the door.

It would be months before Alexandra Kennedy and Will Bennett knew just how right she was.

CHAPTER SEVEN
SUNDAY COMING DOWN

Alex and Will slept in Sunday morning after closing out the night with the hot tub and a last nightcap of Jameson's neat. They had talked about the day and the sadness of Ron's death and all that had to be dealt with and the questions that went with it. And they pondered Jackie's "It isn't quite right" good night and they both had the same unsettled feeling. Something really wasn't quite right. But it was Sunday morning, Will out early for the Times at the Seven Eleven, special coffee brewing and love making for a long time between the pages and the sheets and the coffee refills.

They had just turned on one of the late morning talking head shows when local news broke in with an announcement that a body had been discovered in a toney apartment complex in the Heights, apparently the victim of a stabbing. Violence in Albuquerque was not all that uncommon, although the address of the crime was a bit out of place and neither Will nor Alex gave it much thought. Within minutes the phone rang and Alex picked it up.

"Hello."

Time passed and nothing more was said on Alex's end. This can only be bad news, Will thought to himself, watching his wife's face turn into the game face he had seen a thousand times. No emotion, not even in her eyes.

Finally. "Thank you, Margaret. I appreciate the call. I'll keep it confidential until I either hear from you or hear it on the news. Thank you again." A pause. "Goodbye."

Alexandra Kennedy put down the phone and looked at her husband. "That was Detective Espinoza. The victim in the Heights is…was…Beverly Davis. No forced entry, single stab wound to the heart from behind. The ME puts the time of death some time between very late Friday night to early Saturday morning. Police were called when there'd been no sign of her all day Saturday and this morning. Crime units are on scene as we speak. Margaret said she'll call me back when they know more."

Will Bennett put his own game face on but it was never the armor that Alex could wear, especially with his eyes and his jaw muscles. He said nothing for what seemed like a very long time, just stared into his coffee cup, and then finally looked at Alex still standing by the bed.

"This story is not going to end well, is it?"

"No, not well at all, Will, not well at all."

She crawled back in bed and pulled the covers over them, rolled on her side and cradled her head in the crook of her husband's arm.

Not well at all.

By mid afternoon, the television stations were reporting the victim's name was Beverly Davis, she lived alone at the exclusive Sandia Meadows, and worked as a legal assistant at the Albuquerque law firm of Johnston & Blackwell, PA. Channel 4 noted that this was the second tragedy to hit the law firm in two days with founding partner, Ron Johnston an apparent suicide victim a day earlier. Fortunately, no one drew any connections between the two.

That good fortune lasted all of two hours. Around 5:00, Detective Espinoza called again. She told Alex that there had been no forced entry, neighbors interviewed had neither seen nor heard anything unusual, there was no sign of the murder weapon, and it did not appear that anything had been taken. Espinoza paused.

"Judge Kennedy, do you happen to know why Ron Johnston's fingerprints were all over Ms. Davis' apartment?"

In less than a heartbeat, Kennedy said, "Let me get Will, Margaret. Maybe he might know something." She walked over, put her hand over the receiver and said to Will, "Johnston's fingerprints are in the apartment. Be careful and stick to what you know."

Will felt his face go red. He took the phone from Alex. "Hello?"

The conversation lasted less than ten minutes and Bennett stuck to what he knew. He did tell the detective what he had learned the day before from the staff because not telling her would only put off the inevitable and damage his own credibility to boot. Espinoza told him she would be at the office at 8:00 AM sharp the next morning and ended the call by telling him to have a nice evening. Right, Detective, I'll be sure to have a 'nice evening', his dark mood getting darker by the minute.

When he hung up, Kennedy, who had been hovering nearby, was blunt. "Do you need to lawyer up?"

"Why? I haven't done anything." Alex rolled her eyes. Prisons were full of people who hadn't done anything.

"Will, I know you haven't done anything, but it still wouldn't hurt to talk to somebody. You should talk to everybody in the firm tonight but start with Rita Alverson.

Alverson was a long time friend of Kennedy's and considered one of the two or three top criminal defense attorneys in the State of New Mexico. They got her at home fortunately, and both Kennedy and Bennett were on the call. Alverson listened without interruption until Bennett was finished.

"You know why men name their dicks, Will? So they won't have a total stranger making 95% of their decisions for them. Jesus. Men." Alverson, long single after three disastrous marriages, paused.

"Let the detectives interview the firm. Unless there is some huge secret hiding under a rock, worst case scenario is that

Johnston did Davis in and then went downtown and offed himself. That's got nothing to do with anybody but the two of them. Trying to shut down statements wouldn't do anybody any good. On the other hand, try to get either you or Luis to sit in on the interviews. Moral support if nothing else."

They talked a few more minutes and said their good byes with Rita exacting the promise that Will call her as soon as it was all over. Will found the list of the phone numbers for the attorneys and staff and started in.

CHAPTER EIGHT
CHAOS

The next 48 hours were a nightmare for the men and women of Johnston & Blackwell, PA. Promptly at 8:00 Monday morning, the law offices were invaded by a team of Albuquerque detectives led by Margaret Espinoza. She was accompanied by Detectives Anderson and Mendez and two other homicide detectives.

They had a search warrant signed Sunday night by a district judge and announced that each member of the firm was to submit to an interview. Bennett requested that either he or Luis Moreno be present for the interviews of the staff, and he was told in no uncertain terms that the interviews were to be one on one unless anybody wanted to be represented. In his conversations the night before with everybody in the firm, the decision of each of the firm members was that they had nothing to hide and would agree to be interviewed separately if that was the best they could do.

Outside the Lewis Building, television trucks and camera crews had effectively shut down Central Ave. Somehow the news people had gotten wind of the Johnston – Davis relationship and rumors had fed the frenzy that television news thrived on. And of course the television trucks and camera crews bred crowds of gawkers who stood on the far side of Central expectantly waiting for something to happen.

Will looked out the picture window that overlooked Central, saw several of the spectators point excitedly at him, and he quickly retreated to his office. Not surprisingly, the attorney interviews were relatively short the staff interviews took much longer. While those were going on with Espinoza and Anderson, the other detectives went through everything in the office but for the client files. They boxed up everything in Davis's workspace, everything in Johnston's office, and took the personnel files for both.

At 4:30 PM, Detective Espinoza gathered the lawyers in the same conference room where they had all met just two days earlier. She told them briefly that the interviews were concluded for now, that the investigation was ongoing, and that comments to the press would not be helpful, either to the firm or to the investigation. Phillips and Blackwell both had questions but Espinoza cut them off before they could even get the questions out.

The detectives gathered what they had collected and left. The next elevator up contained several reporters and they could hear footsteps pounding up the stairs.

By prior agreement, Johnston & Blackwell had once again called on Blackwell's father-in-law's PR group who had put together a statement to be read to the press. When the waiting room was packed with reporters and camera crews spilling out into the stairwell, Morton Blackwell read the statement to the masses.

"The men and women of Johnston & Blackwell are deeply saddened by the events of the past two days and the deaths of two very dear colleagues and friends. We express our sympathies and condolences to both the Davis family and the Johnston family and share in their grief. Beyond that, given the ongoing investigation by the Albuquerque Police Department, we have no further comment."

Even before he was done, people began shouting questions at Blackwell. Sorta like people yelling before the end of the National Anthem at the Isotopes game, Will thought to himself. As soon as Blackwell was done, he turned and walked down the hall to the lawyer offices leaving two private security men to stop the horde from invading the inner sanctum. The lawyers followed Blackwell and went to the lunch room where the staff had quietly assembled. Somebody - Will immediately suspected Jackie LaPointe - had stocked the refrigerator with beer and white wine and the women had already helped themselves. The lawyers followed suit as quickly as glasses could be poured and beer can tops popped. Ellen Phillips was the last to join the crowd and came in with her own coffee cup filled with something. Silence until everybody was in the room, everybody took a drink, and then everybody started talking at once except for a couple of notable exceptions that Will found oddly unsettling.

Jackie's words "It isn't quite right" gnawed at him.

CHAPTER NINE
DECOMPRESSION

When everybody got done talking about the time they had had with the detectives, it became clear the cops were operating under the theory that Ron Johnston had gone over to his girlfriend's apartment late Friday night or early Saturday and, for whatever reason, had killed her. Overcome with remorse, he went to the office and had killed himself after leaving a message for his wife, Judy. Most of the interviews had centered on what people knew of the relationship between Davis and Johnston, how long it had gone on, how public it was, how Ron's wife had found out, blah, blah, blah.

As near as Will could put it together, Beverly Davis had confided that she had gotten "involved" with Ron Johnston within months after she had joined the Phillips & Johnston PA firm. She was young, attractive, ambitious and soon taken by the good looking, quiet Johnston. Both of them, so Liz was told the story, knew their relationship was wrong, knew Ron's young kids were at risk, and got involved anyway. Alverson's joke about why men name their penises came to Will's mind and then was chagrined to think, of all people, he should be judgmental. According to the staff, it was the usual 'I don't love my wife, I'll leave her as soon as the kids can understand, I love you more than anything, here, let me help with the Sandia Meadows apartment, how 'bout a nooner, etc., etc.,'. Will had been through it before both as a witness and participant. It was an age old story that had been played out in a million work places and would be played out in a million more.

But, according to Beverly, this one was different. And indeed, some weeks before her death, Beverly had announced to the staff in the lunch room that Ron Johnston had left his wife and the two of them were going to be living together. Both Jackie and Liz confirmed to the police they had been in attendance when the pronouncement had been made.

Why neither Liz nor Jackie had bothered to tell Will was a source of some anger for him, but apparently the code of womanhood trumped all. The room went silent and eyes turned to Ellen Phillips.

She took a long drink from whatever was in her coffee cup and looked around the room. "I can't believe this was going on. I had heard a few things but never thought another thing about it."

As gullible as Will Bennett was, even he had a little trouble with a two person law firm existing for some eight years and the other partner having supposedly no clue what was happening under her nose. He glanced at Jackie and than at Liz and they clearly were not buying this story any more than he was.

What the hell. What the hell.

CHAPTER TEN
SAYING GOODBYE

The next seventy two hours were a blur for Johnston & Blackwell. By Tuesday morning, the police had returned at least the client files, and calls were made to each confirming that there would need to be new representation and that a list of the best real estate lawyers was being mailed to them. Inevitably, each phone call took three times as long as it needed to because the clients, many of whom had been with Ron for years, needed both to grieve and to scold, chastise, express shock and disbelief. Will wondered cynically how many of these folks had their own secret lives for months and years, and that just maybe part of the reaction was as much fear for their own lives as anything.

The firm was advised that the memorial service for Ronald Johnston was to be at 2:00 PM Thursday at the Metcalf Funeral Home. There was to be no visitation. Beverly Davis' Funeral Mass was to be performed that same Thursday at 11:00 AM at St. Adelbert's Catholic Church in the Heights. Visitation with the family was Wednesday evening from 7:00 to 9:00 PM.

The protocol of what the men and women who worked with both were to do was not easy. Tuesday night, Will walked in the door of the townhouse in some haste, immediately made himself a very large martini, and found Alex on the patio with a glass of wine and the paper.

"So, going to Beverly's Mass makes perfect sense. She is the victim of a brutal crime, was loved by all of us, and deserves the respect of us being there." He stopped long enough for Alex to figure out what was going on. "But then having to leave the luncheon early to get back across town to the service for the guy that everybody thinks killed her is…awkward. Don't you think?"

Kennedy was quiet for a moment. "Do you remember years ago that Mary Tyler Moore show when Bubbles the Clown, dressed as a peanut,   got stomped by an elephant in the parade, and how everybody laughed about it in the newsroom except for

Mary who was horrified, and then they got to the funeral, and Mary started laughing uncontrollably?" She paused for dramatic effect. "That feels a little like what you got here."

The next half hour quickly deteriorated into a discussion of what the minister – or anybody for that matter – would say about Ron Johnston given the circumstances. It quickly deteriorated into irreverent blasphemy they were both ashamed of and but loved as a moment between the two of them. They finally voted on the best line: "We always told him he spent too much time at the office." They swore to each other that neither would ever mention either the winner, the honorable mentions of which there were several, nor that the discussion ever took place in the first place. They reminded each other they were both each other's lawyer and the privilege was in place.

Off to the kitchen for another drink and to see if there was anything salvageable for dinner.

The next morning, the discussion around the coffee maker was the same. Do we go to both? Do we only go to Beverly's? Do we only go to the visitation for Beverly and neither service? Little work was getting done around Johnston & Blackwell these days, precious little. About mid morning, Morton Blackwell sent around an email acknowledging the awkwardness of the situation, ordering that the office be closed Thursday in memory of its colleagues, and suggesting that people do what was most comfortable to them. There were no wrong or right ways to do this.

While that wasn't the most helpful piece of advice Morton had ever given, it did give people the right to attend every event in the spectacle…or go biking and skip it all, an option that both Liz and Jackie were seriously considering.

Will decided he didn't have the luxury of doing nothing and opted for both services and the Davis visitation, with a very reluctant Kennedy along for the mass and memorial service and a no show at the visitation.

The visitation was a very sad affair attended mostly by work friends. Beverly's mother and father were both there but isolated from most of the guests. There was a younger sister who was doing her best to keep a smile on her face but having difficulty given the horror of what brought them together. It was an open casket which was something that Will hated. He ignored it and spent the time instead viewing the pictures of a young life now over. There were photos of Beverly in various stages of growing up, high school and college, and pictures with friends. But oddly nothing recent, nothing in the months that Will had known her at the firm, and he wondered about that. He also wondered about who was at the visitation. Or more precisely, who wasn't. During the time he was there, Luis was there, Morton was there, Liz showed up with Jackie, Debra Ramirez, Robin Washington and Ginny Michaels. Somewhat surprisingly, Detective Margaret Espinoza appeared briefly. But no sign of either Ellen Phillips or Jamee Dawe.

"It isn't quite right." He was startled out of his reverie by Jackie's sudden appearance at his side. "No it isn't, but then violent death never is." Paternal, he thought to himself, paternal. Jackie gave him a look that only daughters should give fathers, shrugged her shoulders and walked over to the picture board. But he knew she was right.

When he got home, Will talked to Alex about Dawe's and Phillips' absence. "People grieve in different ways, Will boy. It may be nothing more than that. But weird it is. Let's go snuggle. Tomorrow will be a very long day."

And it was.

Beverly Davis had not been active in the Catholic community recently, and so it fell to the priest who hadn't met her to conduct the mass. Fortunately, Will thought just a tad cynically, they always do it the same way so it doesn't really matter if the priest knows the person or not. Out of nowhere, he remembered his father one time quoting a priest at mass saying liltingly

"Anybody in the house wanna play a game of dominoooos?" and it was only a well placed elbow from Alex that saved him the embarrassment of Mary Tyler Moore. The saddest part of the hour was Beverly's sister attempting to find words to express both grief and anger. They got tangled up quickly and she finally had to sit down uncontrollably sobbing long before she had gotten out what she thought needed to be said. There was no luncheon planned and a small contingent of cars followed the hearse to the graveyard. Will and Alex declined that part of the trip and headed into Albuquerque.

"Did you see Ellen Phillips there?" He asked his bride.

"No, but Jamee was there and that makes me feel a lot better about her."

"I guess."

They had a late lunch at Garcia's and then had just enough time to get to the funeral home for Ron's service. The Bar and Bench were well represented and all members of Johnston and Blackwell, now including Ellen Phillips, were present. But Judy Johnston was not there, nor were the kids that Ron had loved so much. Will and Alex understood but thought it to be very sad. Friends of Ron's spoke of his love of the law and his love of his children, but no one who really knew anything about him spoke and Will was struck by how similar it was to the scene at the law firm when people tried to talk about him. It was like sitting there and watching all the air slowly escape the balloon leaving really nothing to hold on to to remember him. On their way out, they saw Detective Espinoza get in her car. She was by herself and clearly did not want to dawdle.

By mutual assent, and by custom and habit over the years, members of the Bench and Bar congregated back at the Coppertop. Unusually quiet given what had gone on the past several days, nevertheless Will and Alex took comfort in being among their own at least for a while. Alex sat next to Luis Moreno and, after a second glass of wine, he looked over his red cheaters and asked,

"So who was he? Who was Ron Johnston?" It startled Alex that Luis would ask exactly the same troubling questions out loud that she was struggling with herself.

"I honestly don't know. He's been in court a few times, always prepared, always civil, but nothing to write home about. Never have seen him at bar functions or anything like that. I gather he was a workaholic, although that may have been more of an excuse to be with Beverly. Met him a couple of times when they were putting the firm together but he never said much of anything about himself."

Across the table, Will was sitting next to Ellen Phillips and had the same question for her. "Ellen, nobody has really talked about who he was, just what he was. There's like a vacuum where our partner used to be and none of us saw it. Who was he?"

She looked at him for a long time before answering, and he was struck again by what a beautiful woman she was. Movie star looks and she knew what to do with them. Will was reminded of that when she put her hand on his thigh and leaned in closer than she needed to. It also gave him the opportunity to look down at incredible cleavage encased in a black dress and black bra. It also gave him the opportunity to be acutely aware of his wife's presence across the table.

"I guess I knew him as well as anybody," she started, "and that isn't saying much. Even without the Beverly thing, he was always at the office building his practice. He was one of those guys that learned at an early age how to deflect anything that came remotely close to Ron Johnston. Only exception? You could get him to talk about his kids and what they were doing. But when you got done with that, you were done. Nothing about Judy either. It's why he made such a great partner, never troubled you with problems." Her hand ever so slightly moved up his thigh and Will felt his throat drying out. He wondered vaguely how many drinks she'd had and then just as quickly wondered how many he had had. Because one of them had had too many. He looked over at Alex and she was paying rapt attention to Luis. That was a very good thing. He let Ellen's hand rest for a while longer than he should have and he knew exactly why. He liked it. And that wasn't good. She gave his leg a squeeze, finished her drink and stood up. "Long days, Will. I'm going home. See you tomorrow?" Will nodded his head and asked her in a voice not quite his whether she wanted him to walk her to her car. Chivalrous but stupid. She said she'd appreciate it, he told Alex he'd be right back, and he strolled with her to the lot. They'd been at the 'Top for quite awhile and evening was on the way.

At her car, she pushed the lock button, the car beeped and she turned back to Will and hugged him…with a kiss on his ear and perfume in his mind. "Thanks again, sweetheart". She disentangled herself and got in the car. Will turned to walk back into the bar only to find Liz LaRue standing there looking at him. "Careful, big boy." And walked past him to her car.

He went back in knowing how red his face was, rounded up Alex who was beginning to feel the effects of her second Jameson's, not to mention her third, and convinced her that discretion was the better part of valor and that it was time to leave. There had been a time before she was on the bench that wild horses couldn't have pulled her out of there until closing time, but that was one of the lessons she had learned from her colleagues. Drunk judges make for very good reading in the Albuquerque papers.

On the way out, all Will could think of was the ear kiss and perfume. Talk about discretion being the better part of valor.

They stopped and got some take out from Monroe's, got home, Alex went upstairs to change, and never came back down. Will found her under the covers snoring softly and knew she was done for the night. He ate the enchiladas, had some wine out on the patio and tried to figure it all out. But he didn't get very far.

CHAPTER ELEVEN
CARRYING ON

For the first time since last Saturday, there was almost a normalcy to life at Johnston & Blackwell. No police, no reporters, no press conferences, just an attempt by everybody to try to get back to living. Ron's office was shut but the police tape was off. Beverly Davis' work station was empty and still awaiting the return of her computer and other stuff the police had taken, but outwardly everything else seemed as it should be.

Will and the other lawyers made a conscious decision to leave their doors open to promote conversation, and Will even heard Liz laugh at something Jackie had said. She had come in that morning and nothing about the evening before was mentioned. She was there for him when he needed her but both of them knew that about each other. She was very likely not happy about the scene with Ellen in the parking lot, but they had both made so many mistakes in relationships over their years together that neither would ever sit in judgment of the other. Even though Liz thought Alex Kennedy was the best thing that had ever happened to Will and had told him so on numerous occasions in no uncertain terms.

About 11:00 that morning Ellen Phillips appeared at Will's office. If she had been stunning the day before, that had been a dress rehearsal for today. Hair up and back, great pinstripe "business suit" that included a skirt that ended above her knees, a jacket with a blouse underneath that showed plenty of neck and chest, and a diamond necklace, and a well made up face that didn't look like there was any make-up at all.

"Lunch?"

"Sure." Before he even had the chance to think about it one mini second, he said 'sure'. She said something about 'noon', turned and walked away with a swivel that she knew he was watching. Jesus, Will, what the hell are you doing? You love your wife, you've been faithful for all the years together, and it is still the best sex you've ever had. What the hell are you doing? What is it with you? I thought the years of counseling had cured you of this. He took a deep breath, then another one, and then one more. Calmer now, he began to rationalize the 'sure' answer. They were law partners, they needed to talk about the future of the firm without Ron, they had a lot of things to get through. Then he remembered the parking lot yesterday, the kiss on the ear, the perfume, the cleavage in the bar, the hand on his thigh and things went in a slightly different direction. There was an excitement about this that wasn't healthy. I need to cancel right now before anything possibly could happen. But he didn't, and the minutes crept by until she appeared in his doorway just before noon.

"Ready?"

"Sure." Jesus, Will, is that the only thing you can say?

She told him she had to be back by one for a conference call and asked about the sandwich place around the corner. He almost said 'sure' again but managed a 'sounds good' instead. Will was conflicted. The sandwich place was public, they'd be seen and that was good. The conflict was they'd be seen and she had to be back at one.

CHAPTER TWELVE
TMI

They got to Angelo's just ahead of the crowd, got lunch ordered and paid for, and found a table that fronted on Central. Perfect, he thought. Nothing to hide here. Then he felt her knee touch his under the table, got a whiff of her perfume, and began to wander once again.

Saved by the delivery of their sandwiches at least for the moment, Will picked his up, took a large bite, and stopped in mid chew when Ellen said, "There's something I need to tell you, Will." He was pretty sure she had timed it to the second he had a mouthful because there wasn't really anything he could do except chew and nod his head. And her knee was back. Will felt a flush coming on.

"Up until six months ago, Ron Johnston and I were, for a number of years, involved."

Will continued to chew in the hopes they would get to close to leaving time without him having to say anything. No such luck. He nodded his head again.

"It was nothing I was looking for but it happened. It was wrong and I've lived with the guilt about Judy and the kids for a long time, but there's nothing I can do about it. I thought you should know."

Jeez, why? He thought to himself.

"Why?"

"Because before this is all over, it's going to come out and there may be repercussions for the firm, for me, for all of us."

He fell back on his voir dire skills.

"Tell me about it."

"I know you won't believe this but Ron Johnston was one of the randiest men I've ever met. And that's saying something. I think he did animals although he never confirmed it. Anyways, I was coming off a bad relationship with an accountant – never again for that species – and we got drunk one night shortly after we put the firm together and the rest, as they say, was history. He was a great fuck, loved doing it all the time in all the wrong places, the sexual energy in the firm was making us both rich, and he was married and so he was no threat. Had a nice home, a couple of kids. For a long time, it was perfect. I'm pretty randy myself."

There was her knee again. He wondered what time it was but didn't dare look at his watch.

Another softball.

"What happened?"

"He fell in love with me, wanted to leave his family, get married, blah, blah, blah."

Will took another bite of his sandwich more out of self defense than anything else. Lemme see, she's randy, she's sexy, she doesn't want commitment, she's beautiful. Why ever did the dummy fall in love with her?

"Why did he fall in love do you think?"

She laughed. "Will, you're a guy, you should know the answer. Sex. It's what you think about and it's what you call love. It was new, and it was good. And it was a hell of a lot better than he was getting at home. He called it love. The problem was that he wanted it to be something it was never going to be with me."

"End OK?"

"Better than it had any reason to, I suppose because we were doing so well financially more than anything. And he knew I wouldn't blow the whistle with his family. Why should I? So I thought we parted, if not friends, successful law partners."

"How long before Beverly Davis came on the scene?"

Ellen Phillips smiled. "Maybe a week, maybe less. Told you he was randy."

"How did you feel about that?" What? I'm a shrink now?

She smiled again and he felt her knee. Unfortunately ... or not ... his leg was against the table leg and he couldn't move away.

"Ron Johnston was a sweet man, a great lay, and I cared...care...cared for him. So it hurt maybe because it was so close on to us calling it quits. But it was who he was and I think he really needed to believe in love in order for him to do what he did. With me and with many, many more before me."

Bennett thought about Ron Johnston. A quiet man, very good lawyer, good to his kids, and pretty much apparently willing to grab onto anything he could get his hands on. Good looking but no superstar. Small wonder nobody knew him. Too busy in the hunt.

They were closing in on the end of lunch and he needed to ask her.

"So why tell me? It was over months ago, he moved on, you moved on. Where's the harm?"

"Two reasons really. One, I don't think Ron Johnston killed Beverly Davis. He didn't have it in him. And two," the knee hard against his, "I'd love to fuck your brains out."

She got up and headed for the door.

CHAPTER THIRTEEN
TO TELL OR NOT TO TELL

The rest of the afternoon was a blur for Will Bennett. He sat in his office with the door closed and pondered the lunch knowing now much more than he wanted to and thinking about the proposition he'd gotten. It should have been dismissed out of hand with a "I love my wife" closer but, for whatever reason, Ellen Phillips' statement was allowed to hang out there. He did love his wife, had been more satisfied sexually than ever, and had never given a second thought to cheating on her since the day they had become intimate for the first time.

For one thing she carried a gun, he thought to himself. But for another, he simply didn't have the interest in anybody else. Until today. There had been other flirtations, in the office and otherwise, but nothing serious and certainly nothing like what had happened at lunch. He tried to make a list of pros and cons but other than "gettin' some strange", he really couldn't think of anything else that would go on the plus side. Everything else was definitely on the 'con' side: marriage, law firm, future in Albuquerque married to a judge, his own happiness, Alex's happiness, blah blah blah. So that was that. Except that he was a guy, he was flattered, and he could get neither the perfume nor her knee against his off his mind.

So he decided to do the one thing he knew he should do. He would tell Alex what happened. It was times like these that he really missed Sam, his best friend since law school who had been killed by his daughter just months before the new firm had gotten off the ground. He went to that angel on his shoulder and it told him the same thing he knew in his heart, he needed to tell the judge.

With that resolve, he finished out the rest of the day, texted Alex with his ETA and headed out the door. She had gotten home before him, kissed and hugged him when he walked through the door, and asked how his day was.

"Nothin' unusual. Nice to have a day like that after all we've been through." Bennett walked past her into the living room and wondered if his face looked half as red as it felt. Or if his nose was suddenly growing.

She followed after him with a chilled martini up in one hand and a glass of wine in the other. "Hot tub? Drink? Bed? Been awhile." For the first time, he looked at her and noticed she already was in her robe and sandals. By experience, he was certain that was the extent of the wardrobe.

It had been awhile. Trials could be an aphrodisiac and both Will and Alex knew that. Dead people not so much. The last few days and weeks had taken their toll and Alex had picked this night to put the band back together.

"Perfect! Lemme get up stairs, get changed and I'll be right down."

Will launched himself up the stairs, stopped in the bathroom, rummaged under the second drawer of the vanity, found the bottle with the blue pills, gulped one down for insurance, and went into the bedroom to change. He knew he had the time in the hot tub to get things working, hoped the heat and the pill wouldn't kill him, and got into his robe.

Twenty five minutes later, Alex and Will had had a drink, had done the hot tub, and were back into the townhouse. Alex raised an eyebrow, Will nodded, took her by the hand, and they went upstairs.

Later, after the plane had landed, she asked whether he'd taken the 'blue bomber' pill and, for reasons that escaped him, he told her no. He lay next to her pondering why he would lie about such a thing, especially when the honesty of the relationship was such a cornerstone for both of them. But far worse than that was that the lovemaking had been great but, right at the end as the wheels were touching, Will's mind was on somebody else. And that kept him tossing and turning for a very long time.

CHAPTER FOURTEEN
ALEX

She lay in bed next to him, felt him moving this way and that for a long time until he finally fell asleep, and wondered what was up. God knows, it had been a terrible, terrible time so there was plenty of slack to give. But tonight something was just a half bubble off plumb. The sex had been great, but there was something just a little not right and Alex Kennedy worried about it.

From time to time, she would tell Will that she was psychic, that she could see things in the future, that she could read peoples' minds. She wasn't near as good as Will gave her credit for, but still there had always been that sixth sense that had stood her well over the years, that had won her some verdicts she didn't deserve, and had given her a confidence on the bench and with her colleagues that belied her experience. Tonight the antennae were up.

There were plenty of reasons for Will to be distracted, that was for sure. But after all the crap they had been through in the years they should have ended it and didn't, she had gotten to know him as well as she knew herself. Hell, a lot better than she knew herself. And tonight there was something off kilter.

Alex reviewed her options. Her immediate instinct was to wake him up and have at it. A few years ago, that would have been the only option and usually was a story that didn't end well for either of them. So she chose Plan B which was to let it be for a while, decide whether her instincts were on target, and then figure out what to do.

She spooned him as she always did, remembered that other than some cheese and ham in bed, they'd had nothing to eat, drifted and woke up not very many hours later, famished. "Will? Will? You awake? Frontier for breakfast?"

Bennett felt like he'd just closed his eyes, silently reviewed the day ahead and decided there was nothing that was going to take genius legal abilities, and voted for love.

"Chess board?"

"Let's just do breakfast, OK?" Alex was already rummaging the chaos of the bedroom looking for her sweats.

The Frontier Restaurant at 5:00 in the morning is one of the special places to be in America any time of the year. The drunks from the University have gone to bed, the cops are stopping in to get fed, and the early shift that makes Albuquerque work are in stoking up on the famous breakfast burritos. Will and Alex found a booth, settled in on the same side with the paper and, side by side, found their rhythm, their comfort, the oneness one more time.

For Will, it was cathartic.

For Alex, even with all the psychic energy she had, she had no idea what was about to come down. On her, on Will, on the people she cared most about. And even if she had known, there was nothing, nothing that could have stopped it.

They finished breakfast, went back to the townhouse, crawled back into bed as the sun was just coming up, and made love again, this time without fantasies or drugs.

Alex, for the first time in a long time, thought maybe she had gotten it wrong. Except she hadn't.

CHAPTER FIFTEEN
RETREAT

The first of May came and went and the firm was back at full throttle. Everybody stayed busy. One problem was that many of Ron Johnston's real estate clients wanted to stay with the firm that, after Ron's death, had absolutely no experience in real estate issues and, just as importantly, had no interest in learning how to do it.

The good news was that one of the referral lawyers that they were trying to send the business to called Luis Morneo one day and wanted to have lunch. A sole practitioner and a good one, Joe Baker wondered about joining the firm, giving himself a little more security, and keeping Ron's clients. The due diligence after the lunch consisted of some phone calls that were, with one exception, pro forma in their compliments about his work, his work ethic, and his integrity.

The one fly in the ointment was unsolicited call from Rita Alverson to Judge Kennedy. She had heard the rumor about Baker talking with the firm and had called the judge to tell her Baker's wife was a client of her firm, that there had been an initial meeting about starting a divorce, that the two had reconciled, but that the basis for the split had been a domestic violence incident that had taken Baker's wife to the hospital. Alex reported the information to Will, insisted on anonymity for the source and for herself, and held her breath.

He thought about it for a long time but decided the future of the firm would have to trump the troubling news. So Will held his cards, voted for Baker's acceptance into the firm as a full partner, and greeted him warmly.

It would be a short-lived mistake.

Baker had effortlessly moved into the Lewis Building by the middle of May, having been on a month to month shared expenses arrangement with several solos. He took Ron Johnston's old office, empty since his death, and the members of the firm took it as a positive omen that things were moving forward.

Morton Blackwell had a visit from Detective Espinoza indicating that the police were closing their investigation into Beverly Davis' murder, concluding that Johnston had done it in a fit of rage and then took his own life overwhelmed by what he had done. Morton duly reported the meeting to the rest of the lawyers in the firm and all were left with why. Why would he kill his lover of years when he was finally getting into a position of getting divorced and being able to be with her? What kind of rage would cause him to kill her? And like that? But with the closing of the case and the addition of Baker, there was an optimism in the office that had been missing since that horrible Saturday morning in April.

It was Ellen Phillips who suggested it made sense for the group to take a weekend and plan for the future. Bennett, who had studiously avoided any solo contact with Ellen since the lunch, smelled a rat, but the rest of the group thought it made a lot of sense to do a little strategic planning looking down the road. They picked the second weekend in June and confirmed reservations at the Inn at Cloudcroft, a mountain resort that Will and Alex knew well. In the midst of the chaos that had been their life in the aftermath of Sam Greenberg's disappearance and death, they had found comfort and solace at the Inn and had returned from their time there with the stamina to continue that journey on to its end. Will had loved the Inn and was now just a little unsettled at returning there for the firm retreat with the Phillips issue still "out there."

Nevertheless, the group left on a beautiful June Friday afternoon with the blessings of the staff, spouses (Alex had booked a weekend at the hot springs at Ojo Caliente with her best friend and couldn't wait for them to leave), significant others, and family.

After checking in, Blackwell, Phillips, Bennett, Moreno, and Baker met for drinks in the bar and then dinner in the beautiful dining room, kept their promise to talk neither of the law nor of

Johnston's and Davis' death, and instead talked of each other's lives and past. Even with Ellen Phillips across the table keeping her eye on him, Will felt a friendship with the rest of the group and congratulated himself on the choice he had made. He liked Joe Baker a lot and struggled with the knowledge about the domestic violence. Bennett knew rage but could never imagine it spiraling into violence against a woman. He put it in a compartment in his head and let himself enjoy Baker for what he seemed to be - early 40s, balding, and beginning to sag in all the right places when you don't exercise, but bright and funny and seemingly delighted to be with his new firm.

As was the custom, everybody had too much to drink and they adjourned to the deck to enjoy the last warmth of the day and one more nightcap. Will sipped his Jameson's neat carefully, thought of Alex often, and from time to time, glanced Ellen's way, almost always to find her watching him. Feeling like a foolish red-faced teenager, Will was the first to take his leave with the promise they would gather at 8:00 AM sharp for breakfast and then the agreed upon agenda for the future.

Will Bennett got to his room, poured himself one more Jameson's out of the flask he had brought with him, congratulated himself on his bravery and loyalty, got naked and turned on the TV, remote in one hand and drink in the other. Life was good.

A quiet knock at the door.

CHAPTER SIXTEEN
AFTER

Will got back to Albuquerque before noon on Sunday. Alex wasn't home yet and he let himself into the quiet dark cool of the townhouse. Met with reserved panache by Jinks, the seven pound black stray cat that had arrived on Alex's back patio 8 years ago and had never left, Will dropped his bag and collapsed in his chair with a cold glass of water. Saturday had been a good day with lots of ideas about growing the firm, about what people wanted to accomplish, about how long they wanted to practice. There was a familiarity to it that was very welcome to Will after the wars of big firms and he was excited about the future.

Saturday afternoon, some had gone to play golf, some to hike, and then dinner down the mountain at a quiet, very good Mexican restaurant. Early to bed and off early the next morning to salvage what was left of the weekend with friends, family or work.

He sat in the chair for a long time with Jinks on his lap, thoughtful and, especially for him, introspective. Times like this were few and far between for somebody as busy as he was and he relished the time when there was little that had to be done other than be quiet. He knew soon enough Alex would be home, life would begin to percolate, he would gather himself for the week ahead but, for now, a few minutes of solitude was what he needed.

Time passed, he may even have dozed, but with his energy restored, he disentangled himself from Jinks, got up and went to the refrigerator to see what was what, just as Alex Kennedy came through the door. Together, they both said almost simultaneously, "I thought you'd be home later", laughed at that, and then hugged and hugged. Both had left earlier than expected in the hope the other would have thought the same thing. And both had.

While eating a simple late supper together on the back patio, each filled the other in on the time apart, Will talking about the plans for the firm's future that Alex approved of and Alex talking about the time at Ojo Caliente with Karen Stillson. It was a time of peace and love and it ended with the two of them heading upstairs. They read for awhile and turned off the lights, but this time it was Will who couldn't sleep. He replayed the weekend and hoped to God what happened at the Inn at Cloudcroft stayed at the Inn at Cloudcroft.

Just after the 4th of July, Luis and Will tried a plaintiff's wrongful death medical malpractice case in which the allegation was that an ER physician had ignored a number of potential red flags evaluating a 47 year old man who was complaining of shoulder pain after a weekend of uncommon exercise for him and a fight with his wife about his mistress. The man had died three days later of a massive coronary. The defense banked on the fact that the decedent wasn't the best guy in the world and hadn't given a complete history to the doctor, and Will and Luis banked on the two young children he left behind without a dad. An Albuquerque jury sided with the kids and found for the estate to the tune of $2.5 million dollars. Bennett was mindful that you always learn more when you lose than when you win, but this was an awfully sweet moment.

It was the first plaintiff's malpractice case Will had tried in his life, it was defended by his old firm, it was an insurance company he had done work for, and it was clear to Will that a lot of the reason why the case went to trial had to do with retribution on the part of the other side. At the final pretrial, Ralph Woodhull, lead counsel for the defendant and named partner of the firm Will had left, stood up, spun a quarter on the table in front of Luis and Will and their client, Betty Munson, looked straight at the widow and said, "We've made our final offer. You want any more, here's a quarter, call somebody who cares." And walked out. Luis took one of her hands and Will the other. Tears in her eyes. And resolve. "I will do this."

The verdict made it pretty clear that, with this carrier and with his former law firm, he'd be trying a lot more cases and settling less. And that was OK. There would be an appeal to come but both Will and Luis knew the case had gone in clean, that if there were error it was because of rulings by the judge who, years before, had been a member of the defense firm that tried the case, and that sooner or later, as much as the defense despised Will Bennett, they would have to come to the table.

On the way out of the courtroom after the verdict, Luis had stopped at the defense table and spun a quarter on it in front of Woodhull. "Here, I think this may belong to you." And kept on walking.

The firm celebrated the victory at the Coppertop with staff and lawyers toasting the trial team. While Luis and Will got the spotlight, both were smart enough to know that it had been a true team effort. Liz LaRue had done it again in terms of organization of the file and getting witnesses when and where they had to be. Rebecca Jackson, Luis's assistant, had been in the courtroom, had a degree in psychology, and was a huge factor in jury selection and jury watching. But the star of the show was Jackie LaPointe, the so-called "gofer" who knew more about technology than anybody. It had been LaPointe who had put the exhibits together in such a fashion that the jury was mesmerized by the ability by which a push of a button brought to the full screen the most damaging written evidence against the defendant from his own medical records, and the most poignant of pictures of young children who would grow up without their father. It was her work that both Moreno and Bennett knew in large part had carried the day.

Will and Luis were dinosaurs in the technology age but had become believers with the help of this incredible tattooed and pierced young woman who had appeared on their doorstep and had never left. She was a part of the firm and seemed to revel in it. A loner by most accounts, the firm had become her de facto family.

Joe Baker and Ellen Phillips joined the group together. Will, in part because of the trial and in even larger part because he needed to be away from Ellen, had had little to do with either of his partners before the celebration at the Coppertop. Since the retreat, for whatever reason that Will was very grateful for, Ellen had kept her distance as well and there had been no reprise of the lunch. The night of the victory party, it was eminently clear that she had set her sights on a different fish. Joe Baker. They sat very close to each other around the large table, initially joined in the congratulations, and then focused their attention solely on each other to the exclusion of all else and all others. Will noted it, felt a slight momentary pang of jealousy or envy, then discarded the emotion altogether. From his perspective, this ended a very uncomfortable chapter. The couple stayed for an obligatory amount of time and then said their good byes and left very much together. Will remembered an earlier departure from the Coppertop when he had been left with an ear kiss and perfume in his nostrils.

Will would later think he had never seen so many eye rolls in one setting as everybody around the table registered their reaction to what certainly seemed like a "coming out" party for the new couple at Johnston & Blackwell. Will looked around the table and could tell Morton Blackwell was visibly upset. He was certain the next day would bring a visit from the managing partner.

Home by 8:00 and with only a minimal buzz going, he was met at the door by the good judge in her robe holding a bottle of champagne and two chilled glasses. He followed her upstairs discarding articles of trial clothing along the way.

Later, they dissected the trial. It had been Alex who had suggested that Will and Luis should walk to the danger of the decedent being, by all accounts, a not so nice and certainly not so moral man rather than to try to avoid it or soft pedal it. And so they had crafted their case to embrace his failings, put on the table all the hurt he had caused his wife who was also the personal representative of his estate, had her talk about why they tried to stay together in the face of his adultery, and then talk mostly about his love for his children who were the most important things in his life. By those same accounts of his failings was the undeniable and unimpeachable fact that he was an incredible father, a father his children would never see again. They ended with his mistress who told the jury on the day he died, he had told her he had to call the relationship off because his children needed him.

They had counted on Ralph Woodhull's personality of anger in general and his anger at Will specifically to help the cause and they had been right. Rather than realizing what Will and Luis were doing, Woodhull attacked viciously at every turn calling the dead man practically every name in the book, attacking the widow for putting up with him, attacking the mistress for her affair, and finally telling the jury that, in effect, the world was a better place without him. It was serious overkill but the only speed Woodhull had.

The jury thought that while the world might be a better place without him, his kids were a different story. "2.5 says you're wrong, Mr. Woodhull," one of the jurors said to him as they were being escorted from the courtroom.

Having exhausted the trial, Will made mention of the appearance of Ellen Phillips and Joe Baker at the Coppertop. She wanted all of the details and when he was done, she got very quiet. Then finally said, "At least she'll keep her hooks off you for awhile." She rolled over and turned out the light.

Will lay on his back staring at the ceiling for a very long time.

CHAPTER EIGHTEEN
THE RETURN OF CHAOS

Morton Blackwell followed Will into his office the next morning when he got there. Both were early birds at the firm, although Morton usually beat Will by enough time to make the first pot of coffee. He gave Will just enough time to get his cup filled, closed the office door, and exploded.

"I cannot believe what I saw last night. What in God's name is wrong with people these days? Isn't there some sense of decency or do they think it's perfectly all right if the firm gets first row seats at yet another passion play. I swear, Will, these last months I feel like I'm in my own reality TV show except the premise is so preposterous no serious studio would pick it up. We have a dead partner who everybody says was carrying on for years with his secretary, she gets brutally murdered and everybody says it was him, and then he blows his brains out in our office. Then we hire a guy to replace him and within weeks he and Ellen are a public nuisance. Oh, and did I mention he's married too? What is it with these people?" A pause for a breath.

"Why don't you sit down, Morton, and take a deep breath. You're about to cost the firm a new carpet by wearing this one out."

Blackwell looked around, got a breath and sat down.

"They're consenting adults. There's really not much we can do other than to tell them they have to keep their relationship out of the office. But what they do on their own time is up to them, right?"

Morton was silent for a time. "Will, would you talk to the two of them and tell them they have to cool it around here? They'll listen to you."

Bennett thought that was about the worst idea Blackwell had ever had. Picking his words carefully, Will said, "Morton, for a number of reasons, I don't think that's a great idea. I'm afraid it'll have to be you."

Morton. "For a number of reasons, it can't be me, Will." Will looked at Blackwell and hoped the astonishment was hidden by his game face. Ellen Phillips and Morton Blackwell? Yikes, the visual was more than he could bear. She was right. She is a randy woman.

Qualifying for way more information than Will needed or wanted, Morton bared his soul about the night he and Ellen had shared at the Inn at Cloudcroft at the firm retreat in May. He had lived with the guilt and remorse ever since and it was clearly a catharsis for him to get if off his chest by telling Will. But not that great a moment for Will, for sure. The irony of it all did not escape him and Alex, under other and different circumstances, would have found it hysterically funny. Very different circumstances.

"OK, let's do this, Morton. We'll get Luis to do it." The bubble over Will's head was saying 'please, Luis, not you too, ok?' "But maybe we should wait a couple of days because it's possible Ellen and Joe will figure it out on their own."

It wouldn't take a couple of days. There was a quiet knock at the door, it opened and Jackie LaPointe stuck her head in. "Sorry to bother you but there's an hysterical woman on the phone named Ann Baker. She's demanding to talk to 'whoever's in charge.' I'm guessing here but I'm pretty sure this is Joe's wife. Did I mention she's hysterical?" And closed the door quietly. Will was pretty sure she was giggling all the way down the hall.

The two men looked at each other. "OK, Morton, I'll be with you. Let's get her on the speaker." Will called Jackie who was at the front desk and told her to put the call through.

The phone rang, Will pushed the speaker button, Morton started to say, "Hello, this is Morton…" And that's as far as he got. The monologue all told lasted 20 minutes and 38 seconds (Will was timing). What both of them had expected would be a diatribe against her husband instead was a diatribe against the firm. During the 20 minutes and 38 seconds, the gist was that the Bakers were a Christian family with Christian values, that ever since her husband had joined the firm he had been required to spend many nights away from his family on firm business or firm functions, that he constantly told her it was a requirement of the firm that he attend these events or he'd be fired, that he had tried to talk to 'management' and had been ignored, that often times he was away on firm business for two or three days at a time, and that last night had been the last straw when he had arrived home inebriated at 3:00 AM telling her that he had had to stay at a firm party celebrating some verdict that a couple of his partners had won, that he hadn't wanted to stay and drink that much, but that he felt he had to. As she wore down, she again reminded Blackwell and Bennett that the Bakers were a Christian family and that the firm should be ashamed of its sinfulness.

Bennett had been taking copious notes thinking all the while that there was the making of a novel in all of this and trying to keep his composure. Watching Blackwell's face, he saw a range of emotion that started with shock, went to boredom at about the 10 minute mark, and then went finally to anger when he realized that Baker was doing Phillips and blaming it on the firm. When Ann Baker finally ran out of steam, Morton Blackwell quietly told her that he was very sorry about the pain the firm had caused her family and that he would look into the situation that very morning. The phone went dead.

"Well, that went well, Will."

Now it was Will's turn to vent. "If two people want to screw around, I guess that's up to them and whatever moral or spiritual part of their beings they have to consult. I don't sit in judgment when people do silly things because I have done plenty of silly things in my life. But to blame it on the law firm that has given Joe Baker this opportunity of a lifetime is really, really cheesy." Will thought to himself that not only did we give him the opportunity, we also gave him his mistress. What a full service employer we are. "When Joe gets in, let's the two of us talk to him. I'm OK as long as Ellen isn't a part of it. If she insists, then I think it has to be Luis."

"I'll have them tell me as soon as he comes in. Thanks, Will."

Out the door. And back in 10 minutes later.

"Baker called in and said he has an emergency client meeting in Truth or Consequences and is going to be gone two or three days. Phillips called in and said she wouldn't be in today and probably not tomorrow either. Bad flu bug." Blackwell shook his head with a look of tired resignation and walked out hopefully to the sanity of something like doing work for clients, something at least he understood.

Will sat for a moment, thinking about the client list that the firm reviewed before hiring him. Joe Baker didn't have any clients in T or C and neither did the firm.

The rest of the day, the lawyers and staff of Johnston & Blackwell, PA. tried to concentrate on work. Things were a little muted as news of the phone call from Joe Baker's wife circulated upon arrival of the other members of the firm. Only Jackie LaPointe seemed unaffected by the newest drama. Will wondered at the cheerfulness and then went on to other things.

Around 3:00, the elevator doors opened and an attractive but bedraggled late 30ish woman walked into the lobby. With her were two children, a young girl maybe 6 or 7, a young boy maybe 4. The woman's hair was a mess, no makeup and red eyes that had clearly seen a lot of tears. She was clutching a Bible with both hands. Liz LaRue was at the desk and the woman asked to see Morton Blackwell. Liz asked about an appointment and the woman told her that Ann Baker was here to see him. 'Ruh roh', she thought to herself, got up from her chair and went down to Morton's office leaving the woman and children standing in the lobby.

Maybe 5 minutes later, Morton Blackwell walked into the lobby, clearly looking to Liz as though he'd eaten at least one lemon, and introduced himself. Just behind him came Will Bennett who Liz would later think clearly looked as though he wanted to be almost any place but where he was. They took Ann Baker and her kids down the hall to the first conference room on the left.

As opposed to the morning phone call, Ann Baker was composed and quiet maybe because the kids were with her and maybe because she had just worn herself out.

"I am sorry about this morning," she started, "it is just all too much. I know it's not your fault or the firm's fault. I just don't know what to do. This morning just before I called, Joe got up, took a quick shower, threw some clothes in a bag, and told me he had to go out of town for a few days. That's not like him and something terrible is happening. He rarely drank and now he drinks all the time, he was almost always home in time for dinner with the kids and now almost never, we used to talk and talk and now if I can get a grunt out of him, it's a conversation. He would always go to church with us both times on Sunday and now never. Help me." Her hands clutched the Bible so tightly Will could see the white in her knuckles. Her children stood on either side of her silent and motionless almost like mannequins in a store window.

Morton had wanted Will with him for both moral support and to be a witness. They had had a moment to talk about what to say before they met Ann Baker and both thought discretion was the far better part of valor. Neither thought mentioning Ellen Phillips or the scene from last night at the Coppertop would do anybody any good. And so, both talked quietly with Ann Baker about how hard they knew Joe was working to help the firm, had no idea about what was going on at home, and, once he returned, promised they would sit down with him and talk about balance between home and work. Will thought it sounded pretty good.

"Do you think it's another woman?" She asked quietly. Her children showed no emotion or understanding of what she had just asked.

Hating himself even as he said it, "Ann, we all keep pretty much to ourselves here so we don't really have any sense of what each other's lives look like outside of the firm." Hating himself because that statement was simply a lie. It was a close group of people, made closer by the tragedies of the last months and everybody knew damn well what was going on with almost everybody's lives. It was survival.

"Was there a party last night? That's where Joe said he was. Something about a verdict that came in yesterday."

Will again. "There was a party. Luis Moreno and I won a trial and we went to the Coppertop to celebrate. Most everybody was there including Joe."

Ann Baker even quieter now, the Bible now clutched to her breast. "How long did it go on?"

"I left early because I was exhausted," Will said. "Morton, how long did it go on after I left?" Thinking to himself that Morton could pitch in pretty much any time now.

"Boy, Will, I think I left right after you did. Can't do that like I used to." A small smile from the managing partner of the firm.

Silence for a moment. "Who is Ellen Phillips?"

Hoo boy, this was not going well. "She's a partner with the firm." Will wanting like crazy to ask 'why do you ask?' and then falling back on the trial lawyer's creed: If you don't know the answer, don't ask the question.

Ann Baker nodded to herself, stood up, and said, "Thank you for your time, gentlemen. Let's go kids." The two children who had never moved and never said a single word for the entire time, got up and were herded out the door by their mother. Without a look back, she waited for the elevator, got on with her children and disappeared.

Both Blackwell and Bennett let out huge breaths.

"What should we do?" Blackwell almost more to himself than to Will.

"Don't know. How 'bout nothing for now 'til Joe and Ellen are back? "

"Works for me."

"I'm going home."

"Me too."

CHAPTER TWENTY
MISSING

Will slogged home, opened the door, put his briefcase down, went over to the couch, laid down and closed his eyes. Jinks, clearly knowing he needed some comfort, hopped up on his chest and purred. Only minutes later, Alex opened the door with a bag full of groceries, saw Will on the couch, put the bag down and walked over. Never ever does Will Bennett take a nap during a week day, she thought.

He opened his eyes, smiled, and thought again about what a beautiful woman his wife was. "So, how was your day? Or should I make a drink first?"

"Let's do the drinks. I'll get them." He roused himself, checked the bag of groceries and noted a couple of rib eye steaks. Life was about to get a little better. With drinks made, he returned to the living room, the New Mexico sun still too hot to sit outside. Settled in, he told Alex about the day. Years as a trial lawyer and then a judge, she knew better than to interrupt and waited for the end of the story. The only time her expression changed was when Will recounted the part about lying about what he knew about Baker and Phillips. He knew the look meant disappointment but he pushed on.

When he got to the end, both paused and took a drink. Alex Kennedy was a "fixer" and had been all her life. Part of the reason she picked the law was because she could fix wrongs for clients and for her community. Part of the reason she chose to go on the bench was because it gave her the opportunity to fix wrongs. One of the frictions in her relationships with others, including Will, was that she was always trying to fix something when sometimes it wasn't about fixing something but simply about being there to listen.

She had learned the importance of that distinction the hard way, and she knew this time it wasn't about fixing anything. "Sorry, darlin'. Wish there were something to say that would make it better, but these two have gotten themselves in way deep and seem to be taking the firm down with them. Tad selfish, I'd say." She agreed that there needed to be a sit down with the two of them as soon as possible, presumed Will would be one of the people involved, and was not led to believe otherwise by her spouse.

They finished the day off with steaks on the grill and a walk in the park once it cooled off, holding hands and comfortable with themselves. Will had been so obsessed with the office that he purposely made Alex talk about anything but. She told him about some of the gossip at the courthouse (it's always something), a couple of grisly felony murder cases that were coming to trial, normal stuff for a district court judge although not so much for a pacifist civil lawyer. Bennett and Kennedy lived a frenetic pace. Both knew it, both knew it wasn't the healthiest of lifestyles, and neither could or would do anything about it. At least for now. They often talked about a time when things would slow down and there would be more time at Lake Michigan, more time to travel. The problem they had was that Alex was always telling Will he needed to slow down and Will did exactly the same thing to Alex. So they never got any where.

Home to an early appointment in the bedroom. A couple of glasses of champagne, a little Bill Evans on the CD, "and thou". After a very bad day, a very good evening. About to nod off, Alex thought to herself 'there's always been the one thing.'

The next morning, Will was up early and gone, not necessarily eager for what was to happen but to make sure he was there in time for Luis to be brought into the loop. Blackwell and Bennett met with him, filled him in on what had transpired, and Moreno's first question was the obvious one. "Why me?" They gave him the story about being the kindly grandfatherly type and that it would be a much softer, gentler touch from him than from either Will or Morton. Luis was having none of it and gave them both his stern grandfatherly look as though he were about to scold them both for some serious transgression. Then he let it go and girded himself for the task ahead.

Except it never happened. Ellen emailed her assistant, Debra Ramirez, and told her she was still too sick to come in. Nobody heard from Joe Baker. The day passed with a certain tension in the air among both staff and lawyers. Small offices are like small towns. Word gets around.

The next morning Ellen Phillips arrived about 9:00, swept past people in the lobby and hurried to her office. Will passed her and noted two things. She was wearing sunglasses inside and it looked as though her make up had been put on with about three extra coats of whatever it was women put on. And one other thing. She didn't say a word to him or to anybody else.

With no word about Baker, the decision was made for Moreno to talk to Ellen alone. At 10:00, fortified with enough caffeine to keep him up for two or three days, he knocked on her door and went in. Time passed slowly and both Blackwell and Bennett were on pins and needles. At 11:30, Moreno walked out and went back to his own office and shut the door. Within minutes, Ellen Phillips left the office with a bulging brief case and her lap top. Blackwell and Bennett knocked and went into Luis' office.

"After they left the bar the night before last, they went over to her place, had some more to drink, got into a fight and Baker hit her. She hasn't been in because of the bruises on her face. He left and she hasn't seen or heard from him since. She said either he leaves the firm or she will. One or the other. She will not press charges." Luis Moreno was a gentleman and the anger over what had happened to Ellen Phillips was just below the surface. "It's an easy call. We kick Baker out of the firm right this minute or I'm leaving."

Quiet in the office while Blackwell and Bennett digested the story. Will remembered Rita Alverson's phone call about the violence at home and felt sick to his stomach. If he had spoken up at the time, maybe none of this would have happened. 'You chicken shit', he thought. Then he remembered the kids so quiet and docile and wondered if they had been part of this horror. Every once in awhile, you get confronted by the inhumanity of man and the stench of evil can overwhelm you.

Morton said, "Partnership agreement requires a 75% vote for ouster. With Ellen and the three of us, that's 80%. He's gone."

Except that Joe Baker had disappeared.

That afternoon Morton called Ann Baker. She had heard nothing from her husband either and, earlier that day, had called the police to report him missing. Unbeknownst to Bennett that Blackwell had called Baker's wife, Will took a call from Detective Margaret Espinoza asking if she could meet with him as soon as possible about Joe Baker. "Of course, Detective, come on over."

Will called his wife who fortunately was in chambers and filled her in. Her response was quick. "Call Rita."

Good fortune held and she was in. He filled her in on the main points and her response was just as certain as his wife's. "Tell her the truth. There's nothing to hide from your perspective and she needs to know about the Phillips connection. You probably should give Ellen a heads up that this is coming down and that Baker is missing."

Luis called Ellen and left a message on her voice mail.

The remaining three partners met again. Luis looked at his two partners, "Whose idea was it to start this firm anyways?"

Liz LaRue knocked on the conference room door. "Detective Espinoza is here to see Will."

CHAPTER TWENTY ONE
ESPINOZA

"Afternoon, Detective. How can I help?" Will ushered her into his office thinking maybe the picture of his wife the judge would help. It didn't.

"Mr. Bennett, I'm here instead of Missing Persons because of the history Homicide has with your office. As a new law firm, you seem to be developing a very strange pattern of behavior on the part of your partners. One suicide and one gone missing and one staff person murdered and you haven't been in business six months. We find that curious."

'Well, this is a good start,' he thought to himself.

"What can you tell me about Joseph M. Baker?"

Will gave her the official version of the first contact with Joe after Ron Johnston's death, his hire with the firm, subsequent work he was doing. Looking at her notes, she asked, "Ellen Phillips in today?

"Nope. In for a little while and has already left."

"Anything between Ellen Phillips and Joseph Baker that is of interest to this investigation?" Well, that certainly didn't take long.

"Rumors mostly. Ellen was in today and told one of my partners that she and Joe had had a fight two or three days ago and that he had hit her. The next morning there was a message that Joe was going to Truth or Consequences for two or three days on business. We haven't heard from him since."

"Ellen Phillips' home address?"

"I'll get it for you."

"Any problems at work?"

"None. He fit in well here, was well liked by both staff and lawyers, seemed to be doing a great job transitioning Ron's clients to keep them with the firm."

Detective Espinoza looked at her notes again. "You aware that police had been called on three occasions to the Baker home because of domestic violence issues?"

"I didn't know that." Which was technically true. The only incident he was aware of was from Rita Alverson and that didn't include the police. Jesus, what an asshole.

"Kids were involved on one of the calls." Flat, no affect.

Bennett wanted to throw up.

"Any idea where he might be?"

"None whatsoever."

Espinoza looked at him for what seemed like longer than she needed to.

"I may well have some more questions for you, Mr. Bennett, and for your partners and staff but for now I think that does it. If you would get me Ms. Phillips' home address and phone number. Oh," as an afterthought except that Will was just smart enough to know it wasn't and Detective Espinoza was way smart enough to know he knew it, "Mind if I take a look at Mr. Baker's office?"

Will knew this was coming, too. Espinoza didn't have a search warrant with her and he could have denied her request. And she would have been back in about an hour with the warrant and several technicians. None of them had been in Baker's office as far as he knew and he couldn't really think what might be in there that would be harmful to anybody but maybe Joe Baker and maybe Ellen Phillips.

"I certainly don't mind although I would like to be with you just because there may some client files in there that are confidential."

She had hoped for carte blanche by herself but this would do without a warrant.

"Of course."

Together they went to Baker's office. The door was open and, at least to Will, everything looked like it had looked three days ago. Margaret Espinoza stood in the doorway for a long time taking in the scene. Joe's desk with two or three client files on it; a picture of his wife and two kids (taken recently Will thought), a pen and pencil set in front of the blotter, monitor screen and keyboard to the left. A credenza behind the desk and chair, two wing chairs in front of the desk. Art on the walls that were O'Keefe prints. Pretty standard stuff for an Albuquerque lawyer.

She put on latex gloves that seemed to appear out of nowhere and went around to the desk chair. She looked at Bennett still standing at the door, he nodded, and she opened the drawers one by one. Apparently not much to interest the detective until she got to the lower right hand drawer. She paused and then pulled a fifth of Popov Vodka half empty. She looked at Will who just shrugged his shoulders. 'Well, there's a little surprise.' He thought back to times he had seen Joe around the office and the thought that he was a secret drinker had never crossed his mind. He had had his questions about Ellen Phillips from time to time but never Baker. He remembered Blackwell's line about his own reality TV show. No shit.

Espinoza broke his reverie. "Any chance of getting into his computer?"

"It's passworded."

"You have an IT person. Maybe they can help."

Will thought of Jackie. Of course she can help. If it's spelled "computer", she can do it. He thought again of the lack of a warrant and whether there was coming a time when he needed to stop this. But honestly, he was as curious as she was and there was an inevitability to the police getting their hands on it within a very short time.

"Lemme get our IT person."

He found Jackie in her "office" that was in effect a cubicle near the kitchen in the back across from Jamee Dawe's office. She was intent on one of three monitors in the cubicle and had headphones on.

"Jackie?" No response. "Jackie?" Louder. No response. "Jackie!"

She jumped about a foot off her chair. "Jesus Christ. You scared the crap out of me. Why don't you knock?"

He looked around for something to knock on, looked at her again, and got that impish grin from her that told him he'd been had once again. No bonus this year, he thought.

"Detective Espinoza wants to know if she can have a look at Joe's computer. It's passworded."

"Is that legal?" This from a techie who spent several years with the Alexandria Police Department probably doing God's knows what to keep the innocent citizenry safe from whatever. And she wondered if this was legal?

"If not now, in about an hour when the detective gets a search warrant and then you'd be forced to do it. If you're able."

She gave him a look of such disdain that he almost took a step back. She went to the monitor next to the one she was working on, made a couple of entries, and said, "Josephjr4".

Back to Baker's office where he gave the detective the password. "Mind if I sit with you?" Quid pro quo for letting this go on without the formality of a warrant.

"Fine." Margaret Espinoza already past the entry problem. Will took a wing chair and set it up next to the desk chair that held the detective. This close to Margaret Espinoza stopped him cold. Turns out this close she wasn't so much a homicide detective as she was a very attractive woman. Hair well styled, designer pin stripes, good hands, good perfume, good make up. The pinstripes over what looked like a very good figure. Will's mind wandered.

But not for long. "Mr. Bennett, may I help you?" Will's face flushed realizing that he had been staring at the detective's chest and that the detective had been looking at him.

"Sorry. Sorry. Anything?" Why do I do stuff like this?

"I'm not seeing anything here that is helpful to figure out where he is." Just the smallest of smiles on her face knowing she had caught him and at least somewhere in her subconscious being glad she was still being regarded as a woman. "I'd like your assurance that this computer will be locked out and that everything on it will be downloaded onto something we can decipher later. Agreed?"

Will had no idea whether he could agree or not. He called Jackie who came in, talked to the detective, pulled out some little gizmo, stuck it in the computer, typed a couple of strokes, pulled the little gizmo out and told the detective she would keep it under lock and key. Jackie then shut Baker's computer off and unplugged it. Detective Espinoza thanked Jackie for her co-operation, stood, took off her gloves, took Will's hand in both of hers and thanked him for his time and assistance. She let her hands linger just long enough to hopefully let him know his small fantasy was not offensive. And then left.

"You able to track what you just gave her?"

She looked at him with that same look he had seen months ago when she had wired him for a meeting that had gone very wrong back in D.C. It was kind and disdainful all at the same time. "Yes. I'll run through it and get a summary to you tomorrow morning. OK?"

"Thanks, Jackie."

"You're welcome, Will." She turned to leave and then looked back. "Will, I know I'm a lot of things that you don't necessarily approve of. I'm tattooed, I'm pierced, I'm a geek. But hear this. I have never been happier in my life. I love New Mexico, I love this job, I love this firm, and I love all of you. There is something very strange going on here that I haven't quite figured out yet. But I will." And she was gone.

He stood in Baker's office for a long time and then felt the overwhelming need to get to his wife.

The next week went by without any news whatsoever about Joe Baker. APBs went out across the state and then the nation, no sign of his car, no sign of him, no nothing. Johnston & Blackwell PA. soldiered on, clients to work with, questions to be answered from Ron's clients that Joe had taken as well as from Joe's, Ellen returned to work with bruises finally healing and nothing more to be said, a return to something less than normalcy.

A claim of appeal was filed in the malpractice case from a different firm handling the appeal and accompanied by an overture to settlement. Woodhull's firm was out of the picture. The defendant's carrier would pay the verdict with no interest or sanctions and drop the appeal. Moreno and Bennett said they would talk it over with Betty Munson and let them know. She would have taken half of the verdict to have it be over with. Bennett in his head figured out what a third of $2.5 million would mean to the firm.

Margaret Espinoza had called to report that there was nothing to report. Will Bennett was reminded of the disappearance of his best friend when the best of international law enforcement couldn't find him. When you want to disappear and you think about it and you have the money, it can get done.

Still it was weird to have heard nothing from or about Baker. No credit card use, no planes, trains or rental cars. He had simply disappeared.

The police had scoured Baker's computer and had found a treasure of hot emails between Baker and Ellen Phillips. She had been interviewed at length, had confirmed the affair, had confirmed the violence at her home after the victory party, and then held firm to the story that he had left her condo, and had never been seen or heard from again. Ann Baker confirmed her husband had gotten home that morning around 3:00 clearly drunk, had gotten into bed for a few hours, then gotten up, showered and left for Truth or Consequences. Nobody between T or C and Albuquerque could confirm the car, the trip, a motel, a gas station, anything that that trip had ever been made.

Meanwhile, the firm's clients in urgent need of representation were farmed out to the same list of lawyers the firm had looked at when Ron Johnston had died. The firm kept the others in the hope that Baker would resurface but, as each day passed, that hope dimmed. Ann Baker stayed in touch with Morton Blackwell and was living on savings. She was looking for work herself but times were tough and she talked about moving home to Iowa.

CHAPTER TWENTY THREE
REUNION

The first week of August, Alex and Will boarded a flight for Grand Rapids, Michigan via Minneapolis. They had set the week aside for a long anticipated stay at the lake house on Lake Michigan. Will had owned it for years and had decided to keep it even after his move to Albuquerque. It had been the lake house where they had found his best friend's body not so many months ago and there had been a thought that maybe it ought to be sold. But along with Will's daughter, Grace, they had made the decision to keep it. It had meant too much to the family and too much to his friend to get rid of it. Grace used it when she had a break from law school and Will and Alex got there at least twice a year. In the meantime, old friends from West Michigan were always welcome to use it…as long as they left it in good shape and with an addition to the wine and liquor supply.

They got in on time, rented the car, and an hour later were having a drink on the deck overlooking Lake Michigan. It was a view that never failed to lift Will's spirit and he was happy they had made the decision to come, Joe Baker's disappearance notwithstanding. It continued to cast a pall over the firm and, while on the one hand Will felt a little guilty about leaving, on the other hand it already was paying dividends for the two of them. Alex was a New Mexico high desert woman who had been absolutely astonished the first time she saw Lake Michigan. She had never imagined a body of water in the middle of the United States that you couldn't see across and it quickly became her home away from home. Walks on the beach, bicycle rides on the farm roads, quiet breezes off the lake at night, watching sudden storms come across the water were all magic to her.

This week was to be special because a friend from Northern Virginia, Robert Davison, was joining them later in the week. Davison was the Detective Sergeant for the Alexandria, Virginia, Police Department and had been in charge of the murder investigation of Sam Greenberg's wife and the search for Sam Greenberg. Over the course of the long investigation, first Will and then Alex had developed a friendship with Detective Davison that for Will began to fill in the loss of Sam and, for Alex, had been something else she couldn't quite identify. He had been there at the end and since then, they had all continued a long distance phone and email contact. When the trip was planned, both Will and Alex thought of Robert and invited him. His two kids would be with their mom that week so it worked out even better for him. After the divorce from his wife, Robert had been the primary care giver and this would be a welcome break.

They were fortunate to have hit a wonderful string of warm days and beautiful nights, and the first days were made up of all the things they loved about the place. Biking, hiking, dinners at their favorite little restaurant, grilling on the back deck, time with old friends, beach books to be read like the one that was all the rage in airports, *Journey's End,* lots of love making. Neither thought much about work while they were in Michigan and each avoided talking about the troubles at Will's firm. It was John Lennon who said that life is what happens when you're busy making plans. This was their chance to put the brakes on and get back to what really mattered - each other.

On Wednesday, Robert called to confirm he would be into Grand Rapids around 11:00 AM. After some hemming and hawing, he asked if it would be all right if he could bring a "friend". He knew it was an imposition at the last minute but thought it was worth asking. 'Of course' was the answer and they had a third bedroom so all was set.

Will had offered to drive in to get Robert by himself but Alex would have none of it. She wanted to be there as much for herself as to keep her husband company on the trip. They got to the airport in plenty of time, loaded up on Starbucks, and waited at the end of the concourse. And here came Robert Davison with a big smile on his face and Alicia Young on his arm.

Will whooped when he saw her and Alex, feeling some weird pang of something, soon joined in. Alicia Young was the African American Captain of Homicide in Alexandria who Robert,

Will, and a reluctant Alex had convinced that Sam had not killed his wife. It was with her help in breaking all the rules that Sam's killer had been brought to justice. Robert had mentioned that he and Alicia had spent some time together but there hadn't been much more than that.

So here they were. Hugs all around with Alex holding on to Robert maybe a second too long but not so long that anyone would notice. Just carry ons for luggage and they were off. Both Will and Alex were curious beyond words as to what this was all about but bit their tongues for, oh, the first five minutes of the trip.

The judge couldn't take it any longer. "So. Perhaps there's something you forgot to mention, Robert?" He laughed and agreed he might have been holding back 'just a bit'.

Alicia and Robert had been dating now for some months. It was very Q.T. because she was his boss at the police department and particularly police departments frowned on fraternization. Plus Robert was raising his kids and Alicia was raising her murdered sister's kids so there wasn't a lot of time for the two of them to be together. But there was something that kept them in touch and it was good for both of them. The racial thing was a non-issue in D.C. and, as long as they were careful about where they went, they did fine.

The story took up most of the trip back to the lake and both Davison and Young were effusive about the farm country and the rolling land of West Michigan. But effusive didn't begin to describe their reaction when the car pulled around the last bend and they both got their first view of a Great Lake. As excited as two kids at Christmas, they marveled at the colors in the lake and the markings of the sand bars out into the water. They stopped at the lake house just long enough to drop bags, get into swim suits, pack a lunch and off the foursome went to the beach. Will couldn't help but notice that both of their guests had terrific bodies and vowed to keep his T shirt on as long as possible. Alexandra Kennedy, on the other hand, took a back seat to nobody in the figure department even with her "advanced years". Winding behind her husband on the path to the beach, she whispered, "Keep your eyeballs in, Will, you don't want them sandy."

"Heaven. I have died and gone to heaven," Alicia kept saying. She and Robert frolicked in the uncustomarily warm water, splashing and playing like kids. They wanted to make a sand castle and accomplished that with great style and creativity, developing a road way system and even a small graveyard for lady bugs. Will and Alex joined in what they both would later think to be one of the great idyllic afternoons of their lives.

It was clear to the two of them that the relationship between Robert and Alicia was a lot more than two friends having a lark. "They're very much in love, Will, aren't they?" Alex said with only the slightest catch in her voice.

"Sure seems that way, darlin'. Isn't it great?" He was very happy for the two of them because both had been through much and deserved their happiness. He looked at Alex and felt that familiar warmth that was always there. She caught him looking at her and got that same goopy rush. Twue Love.

About 4:30 they decided to head back to the house to clean up and get ready for the evening festivities. They deposited Robert and Alicia on the lower floor for showers ("I'm assuming Robert there is need for just the one bedroom?" "We'll make do, Will. We're used to great sacrifices keeping the public safe.") and went upstairs for their own showers. Maybe two or three minutes later, Will asked Alex, "You hear something from downstairs?"

"Don't start, big boy. You'll get yours soon enough and I don't want you thinking of the beautiful Alicia Young when it's happening either." She laughed but was only half kidding. Young was a knock out.

Just as the four were about to gather, the phone rang. At the lake house, that is almost universally a bad thing and this time was no different.

CHAPTER TWENTY FOUR
FOUND

Will thought for a second about letting it go to voice mail and then picked it up.

"Hello?"

"Mr. Bennett, its Margaret Espinoza. Your office gave me your number. I thought you would want to know that we think we have found Joseph M. Baker." A pause and Will could almost see her looking at her notes. "A bicyclist saw a flash in a canyon on North 14, recognized it as the wreckage of a car and called it in. The Highway Patrol got to it this morning and identified the plates as being the Baker vehicle. There had been some sort of fire and there was one body still in the car. It was badly burned and some animals had gotten to what was left. It will be a couple of days before we can get final identification but the working assumption is that it's Baker."

Will took it all in while the other three watched him knowing this was not going to be a happy ending.

She went on. "It's obviously not on the road to Truth or Consequences and there was no evidence of a briefcase or anything related to work." Another pause. "They did find two fifths of vodka, one empty and the other half empty."

Will remembered the bottle in Baker's office. Jesus.

Espinoza's voice softer now. "I'm sorry, Will, I really am. But if the identity comes through, there will at least be some answers. I let Blackwell know so he's up to speed but I wanted to be the one who told you." It was the first time she had called him Will and he was touched. "I also met with Ann Baker and will keep her posted. It was a little odd, it was almost like she was relieved."

"Thank you, Margaret. Any reason for us to come back right away?"

"Not really. I doubt whether there will be a positive identification before the first of next week and, if it is Baker, time after that for a funeral or memorial service. I say stay in Michigan and enjoy yourselves. Give my best to Judge Kennedy."

"I'll do that and thank you for calling. It means a great deal to us."

"Bye, Will."

"Bye, Margaret." And he hung up.

The others looked at him waiting. He looked at Alex. "They think they found Joe Baker's body in a car in a canyon off of North 14. They'll know for sure in a few days. The body was pretty badly burned and the animals had gotten to what was left."

Alicia raised an eyebrow. "One of my partners who has been missing for awhile."

"Oh Will, I am so sorry."

"Thanks. We were pretty sure it was going to end something like this so it isn't the shock it might have been."

Robert had been kept up to date on the Johnston and Davis deaths but, in the weeks before Michigan, had missed out on Baker's disappearance.

"Here's an idea. Let's get some drinks and snacks, sit out on the deck, and talk about what a great firm you're with, Will." Even Will laughed at the craziness of it all.

They settled in under the shade of the umbrella, wine for the women, a beer for Davison, and a Jameson's for Will. Not so healthy snacks were on the table and were being quickly devoured.

Alex thought again about what an appetite you can work up doing nothing at the beach.

Alex and Will started from the beginning of the formation of Johnston & Blackwell, PA to get Alicia up to speed and ended with the Baker – Phillips tryst and his dramatic disappearance. From the one side of the conversation they had just heard, they knew the rest.

Will got up to get second drinks and when he got back, Alicia took the floor, her captain's face on.

"I've been a cop for too long to believe in random coincidences. In the space of three months, Johnston kills himself, Davis is murdered and Baker dies in a car wreck that involves alcohol and a fire that burns the body beyond recognition. They're all tied to the same group of people. We should think about what the common thread is here and whether there is any connection whatsoever that would tie it all together."

"Ellen Phillips." Will said, more to himself than anybody else.

Alex looked at her husband with a mix of emotions. She knew him so well about 90% of the time and that other 10% was, she guessed, what kept him interesting. To blurt out 'Ellen Phillips' with not a second's hesitation clearly came from the 10% part of the unknown.

"Why Ellen Phillips?" Alex asked.

"She's the common thread. For a number of years, she and Ron Johnston had an affair. More sex than anything, no commitments from either one of them, Johnston raising his family on the side, and boffing Phillips any time they could figure it out. She thought it made for great chemistry. Then Johnston decided he was in love with Phillips and wanted to get a divorce and marry her. Ellen is not a commitment person and called it off. Within two or three weeks, Johnston and Davis were an item."

"And we know this how?" Kennedy now with that edge in her voice which is often where she got when she was in the 10% of Will's mind.

"We had lunch together one time after Ron and Beverly were killed. I guess she wanted to clear the air for some reason."

The bubble over Kennedy's head: And what reason would that be, oh gullible one of the male gender?

"There was one other thing that she said that struck me as odd. She didn't think Johnston had killed Beverly. No reason, just the statement."

Good cops Davison and Young did what good cops do. They listened. Both of them were thinking the same thing. Was Phillips at the center of something?

"How long had Baker and Phillips been together?" As long as Alex was asking the questions, Robert and Alicia stayed quiet.

"First I knew of it was the night we got the verdict. We were all at the Coppertop when Ellen and Joe came in together looking like Siamese twins. They left early and the next day was when Ann Baker came to the firm blaming us for the meltdown in her marriage. If you connect the dots in terms of what she was saying, it had gone on for at least a while. Apparently, that night Baker and Phillips got into it, he beat her up, went home for a few hours and then disappeared. Until today."

Robert said, "Brainstorming here for a second, is she tough enough and mean enough to have killed Beverly Davis because she was sleeping with her ex-lover?"

Everybody looked at Will as though he held some magic knowledge about whether Ellen Phillips was a murderess. Alex in particular had locked onto Will.

"I have no idea. She's a very good lawyer, good rainmaker, big part of the firm. Could she kill somebody? I have no idea. Another woman and with a knife? Geez, it's hard for me to believe. You think Johnston found the body and killed himself because he knew he'd be charged?"

Silence for a moment. Alicia again, "Or did somebody kill him and make it look like a suicide?"

Alex now thinking people were getting a little too far out there. "Oh sure, and maybe somebody got Joe Baker liquored up, drove him up the canyon, and then pushed the car over the cliff. Come on, guys. Really?"

But all the mention of Joe Baker did was get the cops interested in the third death.

"He told everybody he was going to Truth or Consequences to meet clients, except Will tells us Baker didn't have any clients in T or C. And then he disappears the same time Phillips is home nursing her wounds from being beaten up by him. Doesn't that feel a little convenient?" Davison again. "Same question, could Ellen Phillips have killed three people to get revenge for what they had done, or perceived to have done, to her? Wonder how many other men she slept with that ought to be worried?"

A throw away meant to be a funny line but Will hoped like hell that the sunburn from the afternoon covered the blush. He thought briefly about Blackwell. Then he noticed how his wife was studying his face. Going well, he thought to himself, going really well.

"Think I'll start the grill while we think about this." Will rose to get dinner started which, from Alex's perspective, was about the worse thing he could have done.

CHAPTER TWENTY FIVE
DINNER AND AFTER

Will would later think that dinner was a bit frosty, at least in so far as Alex seemed to ignore him completely and spend all of her time on the guests. He even thought she spent a little too much time talking to Robert one on one but then thought he was imagining things.

Dinner itself was superb if he didn't mind saying so. Grilled fresh water salmon, Will Bennett's Famous Fried Potatoes, mozzarella and fresh tomato salad, and a cherry pie for dessert. Afterward, the four of them took a walk on the beach watching the sun sink lower into the water, a beautiful breeze off the water to ensure a good night's sleep. Back to the lake house deck for a night cap and good nights all around.

Will and Alex got into bed but Alex was anything but tired.

"Will, I need to know about Ellen Phillips. I'm not jealous, it's OK if you did her, I just need to know."

Will knew that what his wife had just said was not true but he had heard it enough before in their relationship to accept that she thought it was true. He also knew that truth had been an elusive concept for him when they had first started dating having lived a life time of telling little (or not so little) lies to help him through life's dramas. He had promised truthfulness as a part of their marriage vows and he had lived up to that vow until Ellen Phillips came along. Why do we do this to ourselves, he thought miserably, and then plunged in.

"The lunch with Ellen that I told you all about ended with her wanting to get something going with me. She was pretty explicit. Then the weekend at the Inn, she came to my room after dinner dressed in very little other than to get her from her room to my room. I will not lie to you because I thought about it. I mean I really thought about it. But I told her no simply because I didn't want to have to face either myself or you. She didn't even seem that upset. Said it was too bad, said you were a lucky woman, said if I ever changed my mind to let her know, and then she left." He thought whether the next part was gratuitous but forged on. "I think she ended up with Morton Blackwell that night," explaining why he thought so after Blackwell wanted to duck the meeting with Ellen and Joe Baker.

She listened carefully to him, listened to not only the words but the way he said them. And she believed him. She reminded herself that he had been able to tell lies straight faced in the early days and got away with it but this was a different time. Relieved, Alex took his face in her hands and said, "Let's give those rookies downstairs something to talk about." And so they did.

Will woke up early the next morning feeling better than he had in a long time having now gotten the past weeks off his chest. He went out to find that Robert had beaten him to the coffee and was sitting out on the deck in the coolness of the morning.

"Sleep OK, Robert?" Joining him in one of the Adirondacks.

"Unbelievable. Thanks. You?"

"Same."

"So Will, I've been thinking about your firm and I have a question I need to ask you. You involved in any of this?"

Geez, not him too. "No, Robert, I'm not. Ellen Phillips made a run at me a few weeks back and, for once in my life, I made the right decision. Not easily, you understand."

Davison nodded more to himself than to Will. "Good 'cause I think Alicia may be on to something. We don't think this is over. Tell me about Detective Margaret Espinoza. Any good? Trust her?"

Will thought for a minute. "Yes, I think. On both counts."

"Then the first thing you do when you get back is sit down with her and tell her what we talked about here, OK?" Will promised.

"So on other fronts, this thing with Alicia Young. Tell me about it."

"Will, I love her so much it hurts. I'm trying to balance it all with the job thing 'cause one or both of us would be fired in a heartbeat if the Chief knew and with me being a single parent and with the whole racial thing. But, yeah, at least for me it's the real deal."

"And for her?"

"I think so. But the same problems and worse 'cause of how hard she has worked to get to where she is. I know she's scared that she could throw that all out the window if people found out. Plus she has her sister's kids. So it hasn't been easy except every time I'm with her, I'm whole. You know that feeling?"

Oh yeah, Will thought to himself, oh yeah. "I do indeed, my friend. So keep trying to figure it out."

"We will. Hey, how's Jackie LaPointe working out? I meant to ask yesterday and got lost in the disaster you call your law firm."

In her other life before Albuquerque, Jackie LaPointe had been the techie that the rest of the Alexandria Police Department had relied on for wirings, phone taps (mostly legal, but not always), stuff that nobody else, not even the IT people, understood. Nobody really understood where she came from or where the tattoos or piercings came from or what they meant or who her friends, if any, were or much about anything about her. She had shown a compassion the night Will had been wired because it had ended very badly and it had been that compassion that had won her the job at Johnston & Blackwell PA when she showed up on Will and Alex's doorstep. Will was now of the opinion that regardless of the lawyers' talents, it was Jackie who, somehow, was more and more becoming the glue.

Davison hadn't known Jackie well but was not surprised by what Will told him. "What would she say if you ran this scenario by her?"

"Before or after I call Espinoza?"

"Before."

"Done."

CHAPTER TWENTY SIX
JACKIE

The next two days at the lake house were the best. Michigan blessed them with warm and sunny weather; the four of them blessed each other with no agenda other than to be with each other. Will and Alex showed them a bit of the area, had them meet Rusty and Sue who had become the best of friends, and simply spent time together.

Saturday night on the deck they confronted the differences between the four of them. What a group they made. A pacifist liberal lawyer who hugged pretty much anything that lived, a cowgirl judge who raged against the injustice of it all, a Detective Sergeant getting divorced from his gay spouse and a single parent, and an African American Captain in the Homicide Division of the Alexandria Police Department raising her sister's two kids - a sister killed in a random drive by. There should have been nothing to talk about except they all had the common bond of the Greenberg killing and except that, somehow, they had come to realize there was more to like about how each other felt than the differences. Turned out they had all voted the same in the last presidential race and that, of course, allowed for all of them to rage against the opposition. Now that's a great night.

Sunday morning they all packed into the rental, Will walked the property one more time not so much to make certain that all was well but to celebrate the smells and memories until the next time.

The flights were on different concourses so they said good bye in front of security. Hugs and hugs and kisses and the certainty that this was the beginning of a beautiful friendship. Will made it clear that the lake house was an open invitation, and before they had left, he showed them both where the key was, and where the pump and water heater switches were. Turn key whenever they wanted it.

Alex was going to a judicial conference in DC in September and promised to call them both to get together.

On the way back to the desert through Minneapolis, they talked about the state of Johnston & Blackwell, PA and what Davison and Young had offered in terms of a connection between the seeming unconnected tragedies and Ellen Phillips. On the one hand, there was a simple logic to it. Love affairs gone wrong and the scorned woman's revenge. But there were too many loose ends. First of all, it could well be that Joe Baker had a serious drinking problem, decided to get away for a few days after the fight with Ellen, got drunk and drove his car off the canyon road. That certainly wouldn't be a first for New Mexico. Second, the homicide scene at the Davis murder was ugly and not something that was consistent with anything Ellen Phillips was about. Third, the Ron Johnston scene was about as consistent with a suicide as anybody could find complete with a note, a gun and a reason. And fourth, it just didn't seem like something Ellen Phillips would do even if Baker had assaulted her. If rumor had it, she had been through any number of relationships, none of which had a future. Why would she now be consumed with the rage to kill three people?

They landed on time with more questions than answers, retrieved Jinks at the kennel where, with great disdain, she agreed to accompany them in the car, and then home. There was a voice mail from Robert thanking them both again for the time in Michigan. They were safely home and already back to the lives of single parenthood but with great memories and plans to move ahead – together.

With the time change, Will decided to go down and "clear the decks" by going through his mail. He used his card to get into the elevator and then used it again to get in the office. It was quiet and he moved down the hall to the kitchen to get a soda when he literally ran into Jackie LaPointe who was on her way out of the kitchen.

Both jumped about a foot in surprise and it was all Jackie could do to hold on to a hot cup of tea.

"Jesus, Will. You scared the shit out of me!"

"You? I'm in the old white guy phase of being prone to heart attacks. Yikes."

Heartbeats getting back to normal, Will asked if he she were going to around for a bit and could he have a few minutes to talk to her about the firm.

"Sure, just winding up some stuff," she said as she led the way down the hallway. He followed her thinking there was something a little different about Jackie that he couldn't quite pinpoint. She was wearing jeans and a turtle neck which seemed a little odd given the time of year in New Mexico. She turned when she got to his office and told him she'd been in her office, a reference to the multi monitored cubicle she lived in.

And then he figured it out. No piercings. Lip, nose, both eyebrows all gone. He looked at her hands and noticed a red area on the back of her right hand where once there had been a tattoo of a Black Widow Spider.

"Jackie? What's up?"

He saw her blush a bit and then she said that she had decided to move on to a new phase of her life. Piercings were gone and as she could afford it, she was having the tattoos lasered as well.

"Plus I'm taking the LSATs next week thinking about going to law school. Plus there's a guy I kind of like."

She walked on down the hall leaving Bennett open mouthed and speechless. He took a deep breath and looked in his office.

Will always had that gnawing anticipation of the worst when he had been out of the office for a while but, true to form, Liz had put things into three piles: throwaway, a quick glance and then throwaway, and stuff he needed to look at. There was a fourth pile made up of a firm envelope marked "Urgent". He opened it and there was a note from Liz that there was a check in the firm safe payable to Betty Munson, Personal Representative of the Estate of George Munson, and Johnston & Blackwell PA. In the amount of $2.5 million dollars.

He found Jackie and they went into the breakroom and sat down. Jackie already knew about the check, of course, and smiled broadly. "Keep us in lollipops for awhile, won't it?" "Indeed it shall," Will smiled back.

"So," he started, "Alex and I spent a week at the lake house with Robert Davison and he said to say hi. We talked a lot about you."

"Was the captain with him?" Well, there's a secret well kept.

"Turns out she was. How'd you know about that?"

"Will, it's a police department. Only bigger sieve for information than a police department is a law firm. That's not even news anymore from what I hear. Cops on the force think it's pretty cool."

"The Chief?"

"Don't know, but if he's smart it's hands off. He really want to take that issue on? Doubt it."

Will made a mental note to call Robert when he got home to tell him that his secret had been outed several months ago. It could make life so much better for the two of them.

"So we got to talking the night they found Baker's car." She interrupted with a news flash. "I.D.'d the body. It's Baker. Pretty much burned to a crisp so they did it with dentals. Sorry, didn't mean to interrupt."

"It's OK. No big surprise. Anyways, the Virginia cops wonder if there's a link between Davis, Johnston and Baker. Too much coincidence for their liking. They want me to talk to Detective Espinoza but thought I should run it by you first. What do you think?"

Clearly pleased that Davison and Young both thought he should run the story by her first, Jackie thought for a moment.

"I've thought a lot about it too. Lot of reasons why it makes sense, I guess, except the common denominator would be Ellen Phillips and that doesn't make sense."

"How come?"

Jackie paused. "Ellen Phillips is a lot of things. Some good, some not so. But faking a suicide, murdering an innocent, staging a wreck? I just don't see it. She knows who she is and what she is. It doesn't include that kind of violence."

Will detected just a note of admiration or respect in Jackie's tone when she spoke of Phillips knowing who she was. He thought the same thing of Jackie LaPointe.

"So what is the common denominator if it isn't Ellen?"

"Maybe there just isn't one and this law firm has a black cloud hanging over it. Or maybe there is a connection that's got nothing to do with us. Don't know, Will."

Will told her he would call Espinoza in the morning and asked whether Jackie wanted to come over for supper.

"Thanks but I can't tonight. Plans. Raincheck?"

"Sure." But as they said good bye, he was certain Jackie LaPointe had blushed again when she had said 'plans'.

He turned around at the elevator and said down the hall, "Hey, Jackie?"

She turned. "Yep?"

"You look terrific."

This time he knew she blushed. "Thanks, Boss."

The elevator door open and Will got on. Smiling.

CHAPTER TWENTY SEVEN
ALEXANDRA KENNEDY

With Will off to check to make sure the ship at Johnston & Blackwell was still afloat, Alex was left with some precious time for herself. She considered the various options of what to do with her time. Unpack, do some laundry, check email, or grab a glass of champagne from the half bottle in the refrigerator that hopefully still had some fizz and hit the hot tub. That was not a decision she spent more than a millisecond on. Suit on, glass in hand, she settled into a time of quiet contemplation.

Her mind drifted to the time in Michigan with Alicia and Robert. From the time she had first met him in Virginia some months ago, she had felt something for him. Part of it was that he was a cop and she had always liked cops, part of it was his competence, part of it his compassion, part was his life's story, and part she just put up to chemistry. It was the same chemistry she had felt originally when she met Will Bennett all those years ago and most of which was still there. Maybe it was the newness of meeting somebody like Robert and maybe it was what they went through unraveling the murder of Will's best friend. Robert was seemingly oblivious and that was a very good thing. Will was also oblivious and that was even better. Now back in Albuquerque and with Robert clearly in love with Alicia Young, she put those feelings in the small compartment of a person's brain where you store special memories and fantasies to be taken out and examined in only the most private of moments.

From Robert Davison, her attention shifted to Ellen Phillips and all that was going on in Will's firm. Phillips was one of the most transparent women Alex had ever met and it didn't surprise her one bit that her husband would have been attracted to her. Smart, beautiful, sexy, out there, what's not to turn your head? She knew Will Bennett as well as he knew himself and knew it would only take a little flattery to get him stirred up. But she believed what he had told her and that nothing had happened between the two of them. That was the biggest surprise of all and that he would stay true to Alex in the face of a full court press by Ellen Phillips was a rush for her.

Like all couples she supposed, some of the initial ardor and passion calmed with dealing with the daily agitations of life, although she had precious little to compare it to because her many prior relationships had ended long before this one. Still she loved Will Bennett dearly, knew he loved her, knew there still was the physicality that was big for both of them, and knew most importantly neither one was bored. And now he turns down Ellen Phillips. If he wasn't too late getting home, this could still be a very good night.

Finally, she turned her thoughts to the conversation with Robert and Alicia about the events at Johnston & Blackwell. Neither of them was convinced that the tragedies were coincidental and now neither was Alex. It was just too weird that you could have a murder, suicide, and seeming accident all happen to such a small group of people in such a brief period of time. But maybe. Because if it wasn't just awful coincidence, then there was no explanation whatsoever and that meant that whatever was going on wasn't over and that meant her husband might somehow be in harm's way.

Alex Kennedy had always had a sixth sense about her. It wasn't nearly as strong as her husband thought it was but nevertheless there had certainly been times when her instincts had been spot on. About relationships, about her cases, about juries and now on the bench, many times it was simply pure instinct that would cause her to make decisions that retrospectively were absolutely right even when she did it for the wrong reasons

About to get out of the tub and into a shower, she felt a very cold chill like the temperature had dropped 20 degrees only it hadn't. It scared Alexandra Kennedy to her core.

And it should have.

CHAPTER TWENTY EIGHT
MARGARET ESPINOZA

After a very long, passionate and fun night at the Bennett/Kennedy household, Will showed up for work Monday at his usual early hour. On the way in, he reflected on the night's activities and wasn't quite certain what had taken hold of his wife. From the moment he walked into the townhouse to when they finally got to sleep, there had been some very wild times much like the old days. He had thought about asking and then caught himself. Why would he ever do something like ask why when stuff like this was going on?

If he had asked and if she'd been honest, Alex would have told him it was partly for not letting Ellen Phillips get him and partly the cold chill she had felt that led to a certain desperation in the love making. But he didn't and it passed.

Morton Blackwell was already at the office. They spent a few moments in Will's office catching Will up on what was going on at the firm. Joe Baker's clients had been dispersed as best they could even before they found him last week. A memorial service was planned for Wednesday at the funeral home. Great, Will thought, another weird one.

Preliminary autopsy results of what was left of Baker's body established massive orthopedic and blunt trauma injuries consistent with the accident. Given the condition of the body, the authorities decided not to spend the taxpayers' dollars on toxicology screens. Blackwell had been told that the police surmised that he had been drinking because of the vodka bottles and, frankly, it didn't much matter to any of the living.

"I guess the good news is that because it's an accident, the Key Man is double indemnity so the firm gets a million dollars," Blackwell said.

"Least he was good for something," Will replied. The firm had taken out key man insurance on the partners with the firm as the beneficiary to make sure the firm could continue with some cash flow as it absorbed the loss of a partner. Each of the founding partners had a million in life but Baker had had only half of that for the first year of his partnership. But the accident doubled it. Certainly nothing to sneeze at.

Will thought to himself that if Johnston hadn't killed himself which voided the coverage, they'd really be rolling in dough.

"See any reason we shouldn't bank it for a rainy day? With the fee from your Munson case and with the hourly work holding more than steady, we have plenty of cash on hand."

"Sounds good to me. Maybe when we get to year end we can talk about a bonus for the staff. God knows we've all been through it this year." Will said.

"I'll check with Luis and Ellen but I think it makes sense."

Just as Morton was leaving, he turned back. "Let's make certain Ann Baker has enough to live on. She may well need it worse than us."

Bennett paused. "That's why I love you, Morton. Absolutely."

Blackwell left and Will went to pick up the phone to call Detective Espinoza. Before he could, the phone rang, he picked it up, and it was the detective.

"Geez, that's scary. I was just picking the phone up to call you."

"Will, I wonder if I might have a few minutes of your time today?"

"Of course." Will thought about the mounds of paper on his desk but he would get to it when he could. "Where and when?" He hoped it would be neither his office or the police department.

"Let's do a neutral place. How 'bout Gino's in the Hilton? Say 10:00 this morning?"

"Perfect. See you then, Detective."

"Call me Margaret, Will. Remember? We're past Detective and Mr. Bennett."

"OK. Margaret. See you at 10:00."

'Wonder what she meant by that?' He thought to himself

CHAPTER TWENTYNINE
GINO'S

Just before 10:00 AM, Will walked into what had been a Starbucks back when both Starbucks and the Hilton were seeing better days than now. The hotel had taken it over and turned it into a coffee and muffin place for guests, and workers on their way to the office buildings surrounding the hotel working with the Gino's chain of restaurants in the Albuquerque area. Bennett had learned that a vibrant Italian community lived in the area having come over from the old country to help build the railroad in the late 19th century and, once it was done, had stayed on. Gino's restaurants were some of the best Albuquerque had to offer and had been in the same family for generations.

Margaret Espinoza had already found a table away from the other tables although that wasn't much of a worry because nobody else was in the place. Will bought a coffee and brought it over to the table. He should have noticed, but didn't, that the Detective had taken special care this morning to dress well and make up well for reasons that escaped her.

"Will."

"Margaret."

An innocuous exchange of pleasantries that Will thought was a little like parrying at the beginning of a fight and then to business.

"Why did you want to see me, Will?"

"I was just thinking the same thing about why you wanted to see me, Margaret. After all, you called first."

She smiled at the attempt at humor and agreed the first to call probably had to go first if even by seconds.

"I'll be candid. I don't believe in coincidences. Never have. Never will."

'Yikes,' Will thought to himself. 'Who does this sound like? All cops all over the world and none of them believe in coincidences? Who would have thought?'

Espinoza went on. "Too many people in the same firm with too many connections to be a coincidence."

Will. "Well, wait a sec. Johnston's a suicide, Davis is a murder, and Baker is a car wreck probably in a drunken stupor. How do those dots connect?"

"I know. I'm coming to you rather than my captain because he'd think I was crazy. Three dead people and reasonable explanations for all three. So why bother? APD has a hell of a lot more dead people to worry about that we don't have explanations for." She paused. "But still, you agree it's troubling?"

"I do." Because he did. He remembered Ellen Phillips telling him that she didn't think Ron Johnston had killed Beverly Davis. But then Johnston had sure as hell killed himself with his own gun and left a note for his wife, and Joe Baker had sure as hell run off the twisty North 14 with most of the vodka in the two bottles found in his car in him at the time. Why wasn't it coincidence? Because suicides can be faked and car wrecks staged, that's why.

"I don't think we could ever in a million years prove that Johnston didn't kill himself, or that he didn't kill Davis for some reason. And I don't think we could ever prove in a million years that Joe Baker didn't get drunk, run off the road, and make himself into road kill for the critters. Still. And there is the common factor."

"Ellen Phillips."

"Ellen Phillips. She is the common thread. Ex lover, ex lover's current lover, current lover all dead."

The two were quiet for awhile. Then Espinoza.

"You ever do her, Will?"

'Geez, was that chest pain I just felt?' He thought to himself.

And with a certain amount of smugness, he said, "Nope. Never." And breathed a deep sigh of relief that somehow, someway, he had had the courage to say no.

"Anybody else in the firm?" The detective in her pressed on.

Now here's a moral dilemma. He reflected on his conversation with Blackwell and knew, in the spirit of co-operation, he should tell Margaret Espinoza the truth. But he didn't want to and his friendship with Morton Blackwell ended up trumping the truth.

"Margaret, besides me, and I swear I'm telling the truth about her, that just leaves Luis and Morton." He looked directly at her, took an invisible deep breath, and said, "Really?"

"You're right. Of course. As long as you're telling the truth about you. You do have a certain reputation that came with you to New Mexico, you know."

There had been that one time when he and Alex had been on the outs that things had gotten 'mushy' up in Michigan before they had put the band back together, but Bennett was astounded that Espinoza knew about it.

"Why do you say something like that, Detective?"

"This is a very small town, Mr. Bennett. Word gets around. You know what they say, rumors don't matter if they're true. Just so long as you repeat them." A smile. "Alexandra Kennedy has a lot of friends in this town. They worry about her."

"I'm telling the truth this time, Margaret." With the emphasis on 'this time.'

"I assume you all have key man? Tell me about it."

Bennett paused trying to get his head around the sudden shift in the questioning and realizing that this is where Espinoza had wanted to be all along.

"We do. A million on each partner except for half a mill on Baker with the beneficiary being the PA."

"So how is the firm doing with the bodies piling up?" There was now an edge to her voice that was very unsettling to Will and he for sure did not like where this was going. A long pause. He tried staring her down but got nowhere. Although he thought she had beautiful brown eyes when you really looked at them.

"Johnston's suicide was an exclusion. We didn't get it on our staff. And the firm is set to collect a million on Baker – half a mill on the policy with double indemnity for the accidental death."

Now it was her turn to pause. "Out of curiosity, if everybody is dead except for the last partner, does **he** get it all?" Big emphasis on the 'he'.

"Honestly, I haven't really thought about it," he said. Because truthfully he really hadn't thought about it.

"So if you and I don't believe in coincidences, and if Johnston's death wasn't suicide and Baker's death wasn't an accident, aren't you, Blackwell, Phillips and Moreno sort of suspects?"

Fuck.

CHAPTER THIRTY
LAWYERING UP

Will Bennett was just smart enough to know that Margaret
Espinoza had done her homework and had set a trap based on the
last one standing if there were no such thing as a coincidence. He
pushed back from the table.

"Nice speaking with you, Detective."

"You too, Mr. Bennett. I'll be in touch." They pro forma
shook hands and again Bennett was struck by how attractive the
detective was even in the midst of her almost accusing him and the
surviving members of the firm of murder.

He went back to the office and called his wife. Fortunately,
she was in chambers and could take the call. He went through the
meeting with Espinoza and when he was done they both, almost in
the same breath, said the same thing. "Rita."

Rita Alverson met Will for lunch in a little green chili
cheeseburger place south of town.

"Thanks for the short notice, Rita."

"My pleasure, Will. I owe your wife a lot. What can I
do?"

"Well," big drink of iced tea, "Here's where we stand."

This time he left nothing out. Forty five minutes later he
had exhausted his recitation of the facts and his own emotional
reservoir ending with his most recent meeting with Detective
Espinoza. His lawyer had said nothing the whole time and had
taken just a very few notes on a small pad. When he was done, she
put her pen down and looked at him for a time that, to Will,
seemed like forever.

"I will never tell Alex, Will, but I really need to know. You and Ellen Phillips. Past, present or future. I really need to know this."

"I swear, Rita, since I've been with Alex, I get it. There were opportunities with Ellen, I can't deny that." The knock on the door at the Inn at Cloudcroft and the uncomfortable conversation that followed in the doorway of his room came to mind. "But I swear it didn't happen."

She continued to look at him without blinking.

Finally. "OK, this is what I'm thinking. You're done talking with cops without first telling me they want to talk to you and making certain I'm present from here on out. Understood?" Bennett nodded. "Tell Moreno and Blackwell they need to lawyer up and give them the same instruction. No interviews with the police without counsel. Understood?" He nodded again.

"Should I tell Phillips the same thing?"

Rita Alverson was silent for awhile. "Will, I can't tell you why but I don't think you should say anything to her. I agree with Detective Espinoza that there's no such thing as coincidence until it's proven beyond a reasonable doubt. And here, God knows, there's plenty of doubt, reasonable or not. If it is coincidence and you are a member of the unluckiest law firm in the history of the profession saying anything to her won't change that. If it isn't coincidence, Ellen Phillips is the glue that holds this all together. Telling her to lawyer up only makes her go underground."

Now it was Will's turn to go silent. Then. "Do either Luis, Morton or me have anything to worry about in terms of our own health and well being?"

"Will, you know the answer to that already. If you're not a murderer and what's happened to the others was neither random, suicide, or an accident, and if there's another $4 mill out there in key man life insurance, three of you are in danger." She said it so matter of factly that she might have been talking about her plans for the weekend but even so, it struck a very bad nerve in her client. He hadn't really thought about his own safety because until Espinoza had asked about the key man, he had assumed the best case was coincidence and the worst case had to do with Ellen Phillips and her lovers. And he had avoided that particular issue. Barely avoided, he knew, but still avoided. But if the larger plot wasn't jilted lovers but millions of dollars to the survivor of the law firm, he could be in somebody's cross hairs.

Lunch over, Will paid and walked Rita out to the parking lot. As she opened the door of her car, she looked at him again. "I believe you, Will, about Ellen Phillips. The judge is a lucky woman." Will thanked her, she got in her car, and left Will in the lot pondering. He finally moved to his car but surveyed the lot carefully before he got in, wondering about whether there was somebody else on somebody's list.

Driving back to the office, he considered Morton Blackwell, Luis Moreno and Ellen Phillips in a whole new light. Luis he just couldn't see somehow involved in a horrible plot to kill his partners for money. He gave away most of the money he did make. Why the hell would he kill off his partners to make more? Morton Blackwell? Again Will came up short. Well to do, good lawyer, always wanting to do the right thing, and a hand wringer over every penny spent at the office. Again, not a match.

But Ellen Phillips made him nervous and he tried to figure out why. There was the obvious, of course. The connection between her and Ron Johnston, the connection once removed between her and Beverly Davis, and the connection between her and Joe Baker could conjure up motive, but it would have nothing to do with key man life insurance. Worst case scenario, she was a black widow spider and Beverly Davis was collateral damage. Plus Will hadn't done her so he should be in the clear. Unless of course not doing her was motive enough for her. He thought Blackwell had more to worry about than him but it still stuck with him.

CHAPTER THIRTY ONE
NORMALCY

When Will got back to the office, he found Morton and Luis and told them he wanted to see them after work at the townhouse in Old Town. Ellen Phillips was at a client meeting which was a good thing. Will called his wife who was on the bench and left her a voice mail summarizing the lunch with Rita, and telling her he was meeting his partners at the house and asking for a reprieve until 6:30. For the next three hours he found solace in the mundane world of the practice of law, returning emails that had stacked up, checking with Liz about depositions that were being scheduled in another med mal case, and going over some discovery responses that needed to be finalized before going to the client for her signature.

At 4:30 he left the office, picked up some chips and dip, and at 5:00 sharp, Blackwell and Moreno knocked on the door. He got them their drinks of choice and they adjourned to the patio where Will filled them in first on his conversation with Detective Espinoza, and then on the advice by Rita for both of them to lawyer up. Neither seemed surprised at the advice but both had seemed taken aback by the reference to the key man life insurance. Blackwell was the first to speak.

"Who in their right mind would kill off all the partners leaving only themselves standing? Wouldn't that be sort of obvious to the police if everybody dies in a mysterious way? I'm not buying it. I think Ellen is doing lovers and lovers' lovers." He suddenly stopped and his face froze almost with his mouth still open on the last 'lovers'. He looked at Will and it was apparent that he now put himself in one of those categories. Will saw Morton's face lose all color even in the afternoon shade. The managing partner attempted a recovery.

"But that's insane. Ron is lying at his desk with gun in hand, Beverly Davis is killed by somebody in a homicidal rage, and Joe Baker probably has enough vodka in him to stock the

Coppertop. We're starting to see boogey men where there aren't any." But he didn't seem real convinced.

Moreno's turn. "I agree with my friend, Morton. We're snake bit, shit comes in threes and we've had our three. Time to move on. I don't need a lawyer. But I do need another drink." And moved inside to fix himself up.

While he was inside, Blackwell looked at Will. "Do you think I'm next? Jesus Christ, Will, what am I gonna do?"

"I really think talking this through with a lawyer makes sense, Morton. Just in case."

Luis joined them back on the porch and they talked of more mundane things about the office and how the firm was doing.

Blackwell asked if they should "do anything about Ellen".

"Like what, Morton," Luis asked. "We're going to fire her because of a murder, a suicide, and an accident? What an interesting discrimination case that would be." Sarcasm was not Moreno's strong suit but his partners got the point. "Let's just get on with doing what we do best, OK?" And with that, the party was over.

Will thanked them both for coming over and thought again how fortunate he was to be in partnership with them. They drove away just as Alex drove in.

She got out, surveyed the situation, announced there was nothing in the whole house to eat and that they were going to Seasons for dinner. Will figured her for either one Jameson's or two splits of champagne before she got home. He knew her that well. He got his suit coat and followed her down the street. They spent the dinner in conversation about the day and what to do next. At the end, they both decided there was nothing to do other than what they had put in place. Will asked his wife about him buying a gun and once again, as in all the other times he had asked the question, she adamantly prohibited him from ever voicing that thought again. Will Bennett with a gun in his hand was a story that would only end badly, most probably for Will who would surely accidentally kill himself with it before he hit anything else. Conversation over. "Besides, if you and Ellen never got it on, what's the worry?" So be it.

The next morning Detective Espinoza called the office to set up interviews with Luis Moreno and Morton Blackwell, and both agreed to meet with her without counsel. Will felt like he ought to bill them for their drinks the night before for all the good his advice had done. She also wanted to talk with Ellen Phillips who did refuse unless she had an attorney and that would take several days to set up.

The interviews went off that morning and both Moreno and Blackwell reported they had gone fine. The lingering question for Will was whether Morton had told the detective about his tryst with Ellen Phillips at Inn at Cloudcroft and, if so, whether he had told the detective that Bennett was aware of it. That wouldn't be a good thing.

At the end of the day, Morton gathered the firm together and filled them in on what had gone on with the interviews. Needless to say, it had been the only topic of conversation among the staff for the entire day. As best he could, he attempted to calm the waters, but it was Jamee Dawe who uncharacteristically spoke up and talked of the quality of the people at the firm, the friendships that had been forged, and the need to stick together through these most difficult of times. Will immediately thought she needed to get to law school and become a trial lawyer. She ended with this:

"We are family."

CHAPTER THIRTY TWO
DC

The week after Labor Day, Alex packed for the State Judicial Conference in Washington, D.C. Every four years judges gathered from all over the country for five days to discuss various and sundry issues peculiar to the state courts, to meet new colleagues and renew old acquaintances, to hear a boring speech from one of the Supreme Court Justices, and overall, to eat and drink too much. Perk of the job.

This was the second of these that Judge Kennedy had attended. The first had been in Las Vegas and she had come home a day early exhausted from the bullshit laid down by too many of her peers who suffered badly from "Robeitis", a little known syndrome caused apparently be simply putting on the black robes of the judiciary. This time she looked forward to the trip, but only because she had been in touch with Robert Davison with whom she had planned on at least a dinner and maybe an afternoon if she could get away. To her delight, Alicia could not join them having already committed to an outing with her sister's children over the weekend.

She packed with care pulling out some of her nicest (and sexiest) clothes and making certain that make up and accessories were also on board. Even Will, usually clueless about matters of the heart, recognized the excitement in the run up to leaving.

"I thought you hated these things, Alex."

"You know I do, Will, but it will be good to see some of the people again and I was even thinking about taking some time to get to the art galleries and museums. Plus this is such a much better trip than the last time we were there," alluding to the horror that had been the Greenberg deaths and investigation.

For Will Bennett, never seeing either the Capitol or Northern Virginia again was a priority, but Alex had been a step removed from all that had gone on there. He understood that and let it go.

That Thursday morning he took Alex to the airport, kissed her good bye, told her the flights were guaranteed and that he loved her very much. He drove away trying to remember if she had said she loved him.

Unbeknownst to Will, Alex had booked a room at the Holiday Inn in Alexandria, Virginia just across the Potomac River from Washington. She did it primarily because of the memories there when she and Will and Robert had put together the plan to find Sam Greenberg's killer and to be away from the madding crowds of judges who would be amassing at the hotel where the conference was being held. Nothing worse than being around hundreds of drunk judges, she rationalized.

She got in on time, checked into the hotel, called Will to tell him she was safe and then, uncharacteristically breathless, called Robert. They agreed to meet the next night for dinner and Robert said he would pick her up at 7:00 at the hotel.

The first day of the judicial conference seemed like it would never end, and Kennedy spent most of the day wondering why time went so slowly when you were waiting for the time to pass and so quickly when you weren't. She attended various break out sessions, none of which she remembered minutes after she left, had lunch with the women judges in attendance that was significantly higher in number than even four years past and endured a long dreary afternoon of speakers presenting on such diverse topics as sexual harassment in the courtroom to security for the judges and whether they should carry guns on the bench.

Finally it was over and Alex, begging off two or three offers to have dinner, cabbed it back to Alexandria. A hot bath, fiddling over what to wear, and then spending way more time than she usually did on make up. She wondered vaguely about what she was feeling and why. Was it a throwback to her younger years when she would leave boyfriends by the scores discarded on a whim? Was it trying to remember that forgotten youth and wondering where the time had gone? She looked at herself and felt what? Pretty? Attractive? The phone rang and Robert was in the lobby.

She took one more look in the mirror, wondered if there was too much cleavage, and then figured it was too late to do anything about it, turned the key and left. Only walking down the hall to the lobby did she remember she hadn't spoken to Will at all that day. When I get home, she thought. Time difference will help.

Robert's reaction when she walked into the lobby was exactly what she had hoped for.

"Wow. Alex, you're stunning! Don't think I've ever seen you look so…so…"

She hugged him and gave him a kiss on the cheek that was closer to his ear than it should have been.

He took her to a small Italian restaurant not far from the hotel. Unlike the agony of the judicial conference when every second seemed like an hour, the night flew by. Almost by design on both of their parts, little time was spent on either Alicia or Will. Mostly they talked about their backgrounds and their jobs and laughed a lot. She caught him several times looking at her cleavage and wondered again if it was a little much. She had committed herself to only two drinks and managed to accomplish that plus a glass of wine, or maybe it was two, at dinner. She knew having too much to drink was a recipe for disaster but, what was the line? Everything in moderation including moderation.

They left the restaurant and headed back to the hotel.

"It's still early, Robert. Time for a nightcap?"

"Sure, Alex. Sounds good." She couldn't tell if he were feeling the effects of the alcohol or not but he seemed fine and that was enough for her. The bar was empty save for a few regulars and they found a booth towards the rear.

Halfway through her Jameson's neat, Alex Kennedy took a deep breath, looked at Robert, held his eyes for a minute and said, "Robert, I really would like to make love to you tonight."

For the second time that day, time also stopped. Robert Davison never took his eyes off Alex for what seemed like an eternity.

CHAPTER THIRTY THREE
LOST IN AMERICA

The next morning, Alex Kennedy packed her bag, checked out of the hotel two days early, took a cab to National Airport, rented a car with GPS and headed west. She told no one at the conference she was leaving. She just left.

Shame, humiliation, embarrassment, anger, even relief all became one glob of awful emotion that consumed her as the miles rolled by. Other than gas breaks and pee stops, she drove without a break. Day turned to twilight and then darkness and she continued on. At 2:00 AM, she pulled into a Best Western in Tulsa, registered and fell into bed, once more reliving those awful moments from the night before.

Without a word Robert had put enough money on the table for the drinks, they both stood up and he followed her to the elevator. Once in, Alex pushed Three and they silently watched the elevator numbers go from One to Two to Three. The doors opened and Alex stepped off. They turned and looked at each other and, in absolute unison, said "I can't do this." Startled, they looked at each other and then both laughed on cue.

"Robert, I'm so sorry. I have no idea what I was thinking."

"No worries, Alex. Thanks."

They hugged each other, Robert pushed the down button and thankfully the doors immediately opened and he got on. They waved good bye as the doors shut.

She lay in bed that night and never slept. What the fuck was I thinking? What's he thinking? Who am I? About 3:00 AM, she sat straight up in bed. What if he tells Will? And it was that question that led her to make a run for it.

Alex Kennedy woke up at 10:00 AM with a thousand miles between her and the Alexandria Holiday Inn. Her first conscious thought: Judges don't get rejected, they get appealed. And smiled to herself for the first time. At least they had both stopped it at the same time and for that she was grateful. She remembered she hadn't spoken to Will at all yesterday. She called him, thankfully got his voice mail, told him the conference was going fine, she had had dinner with Robert that was nice (Jesus, has he already called Will and told him?), was off for another full day at the conference and then home on schedule, loved him very much, and was really looking forward to getting home. She hung up and wondered again about Robert.

Breakfast on board and off again for another day of watching America roll by. Somewhere around Oklahoma City, she began to pull herself together. Ok, it was really stupid and but for the alcohol, probably wouldn't have happened at all. Except she had been attracted to Robert ever since the investigation into Sam Greenberg's death. So maybe it was inevitable. But it wasn't like she hadn't planned it from the judicial conference trip to packing just the right things, to dressing just right for dinner. It was the premeditation that scared her because that had nothing to do with alcohol. But it had stopped short of what it could have been.

And what about Will? She loved him more than she had loved anybody. Why risk all of that with his friend? If she really wanted some strange, she could have done it with a lot less risk. What a tramp. What to tell Will? Did he already know? If not, should he know anyways? There was the honesty thing that had taken a long time to work out and now she herself was faced with the dilemma of truth AND consequences? Or neither? Besides, nothing had happened, so why feel guilty? Alex decided to play it by ear.

Some hours later, she pulled off into a rest area and called Will. They talked for a good while and Alex filled him in on the fiction of the judicial conference that she had left two days ago and her dinner with Robert in which he had told her how much in love he was (at least that part was the truth). He sounded fine and Alex felt a sense of relief that maybe, just maybe, Robert hadn't called him. Right before they were done, Will asked her whether John

Thorogood was at the conference, a question that stopped Alex in her tracks. Thorogood was a judge in Gallup and for many years had been a Same Time Next Year lover for Alex. She had told Will about him as a part of the honesty program when they had first gotten serious but it had ended long before Will came on the scene. Where the hell did that come from? Fortunately, he had not been there and she told him so. But it was unsettling to her that he would ask that question at this time. They said good bye with Alex still wondering.

Alex arrived back in Albuquerque the next day with several hours to spare before her plane would have arrived from DC via Dallas. She turned in the car, hung around the airport until the appropriate time and then got a cab. Halfway to the townhouse, her cell phone rang.

Will. "Hey. Where are you? Thought I'd surprise you and pick you up."

Shit.

That night over cocktails and dinner at Seasons, they tried to figure out how they had missed each other, laughed it off, and seemed back to normal. Either Will was a better actor than she thought or Robert hadn't called. She saw no reason in the world why she should confess to something that didn't happen. Hell, everybody fantasizes, right?

That night, Alex feigned fatigue as an excuse not to make love but held Will as close to her as she could. And the next morning loved him as much as she could.

CHAPTER THIRTY FOUR
IS IT FINALLY OVER?

And then the noise stopped for awhile. Late summer and early fall the firm of Johnston & Blackwell continued to exist and prosper. Months later Will would look back on this time as being almost surreal especially knowing then how it would all end. They stabilized with the four partners and staff and each practiced law within their specialties. There was an undercurrent of tension with Ellen Phillips that never quite went away. She came to work every day, continued to rain make, talked about adding another lawyer to her practice, but never once brought up Johnston, Davis or Baker. Indeed, she became almost a recluse socializing only when necessary with her partners and the staff. While in many ways it was off putting, her male partners in fact were overjoyed.

Will's life was a series of depositions, lay and expert, preparing for the next big case, a business dissolution that was worse than any divorce Will had ever heard of. The two brothers, Ray and Clarence Barnes, had taken over their parents' very successful business of designing and manufacturing dental implants and promptly had a bitter falling out that resulted in litigation to sell the company and divide the spoils.

Both Will and his counterpart had tried to counsel their respective clients that litigating what in the end would not be a lot of money after splitting it two ways was a stupid use of resources, but neither brother would budge. Millions for defense, blah, blah, blah. Will at one level thought that having a client with more money than brains was probably a good thing but the hatred and anger was exhausting. In mid October with a November trial date pending, the trial judge ordered the case to mediation and ordered that former district judge Rebecca Sitterly mediate it. A full day went by and little was accomplished other than the expected yelling and screaming, but Judge Sitterly left the parties with a mediator's number to either accept or reject. And whether it was because it was her number and neither of the brothers', or whether each had gotten another heavy bill from their lawyers, both agreed to the number and the case suddenly was over. Will wonders never cease?

Suddenly Will had nothing to do with the two and a half week block - the second and third weeks bumping up against Thanksgiving - that he had set aside for the trial. Normally, he would rush around like a mad man and try to fill the gaps in. But this time would be different. Between the paying clients coming in the door and paying their bills, the key man life insurance for Baker, and the verdict in the Munson case, the firm was, for lack of a better word, having a very successful year. Very.

He got home from the mediation and told Alex about the settlement. For only a split second, she hesitated and then laughed that wonderful laugh. "Well, here is a coincidence. That banger who was going to trial for murder one in November? He pled today. Case over. No trial in November."

The next day, Will announced to his partners that he and Alex were taking a two week vacation to Europe over Thanksgiving unless anybody had any objections. Nobody did and Alex, Will and Liz went into action. One of Liz's many positives was that she was an absolute whiz at bargain hunting. She found an apartment in the Le Marais district of Paris and booked them there for 10 days at an astonishingly low rate. Alex and Will found a three day bicycle wine trip in the Provence Region in the south of France that should still have OK weather, and also some day trips from Paris. They both agreed this would be a balance between drinking coffee at French cafes, people watching, and love making, and some excursions to museums. Will was more into the former and less the latter and Alex vice versa, but the compromise plan satisfied them both.

The next two weeks were a whirlwind with Will and Liz shutting down the trial machine and preparing complicated settlement documents for Mr. Barnes and doing what else needed to be done for that long a time away. She announced that she and her boyfriend would also take advantage of the lull and had booked a week at a resort in California, clothes optional. She was a year younger than Will and in great shape since moving to New Mexico, but the thought of her spending a week at a "clothes optional" resort was simply TMI. He told her he hoped they would have a great time and silently hoped she wouldn't take a camera. Or at least not bring it back to the office.

They were like kids before the first week in school. Both went travel shopping and Will found some underwear that advertised it was the only pair he would need for six weeks of hard travel ("Please, Will, for me. Get more than one pair"); they both bought wash and wear clothes; they bought the newest version of Kindles to travel more efficiently, although Will would miss the tactile feel and sensation of page turning; they bought Kindle maps and tour books of Paris and France for things to do. Why? All to avoid having to pay to check bags. Both Will and Alex had a finely tuned sense of justice and one of the things that frosted them like nothing else was the concept of buying expensive tickets to sit in long aluminum sardine cans, being given nothing to eat and barely anything to drink, and then having to pay a ridiculous amount of money to check bags. So like many, many other travelers, they chose to revolt. Check in was no quicker because of all of the luggage people were carrying on and customs was slower because it all had to be checked but there it was, the little person doing what they could to take a stand.

Albuquerque to Chicago to DeGaulle overnight and they were there. An expensive taxi ride to Le Marais and they found their apartment at about 8:00 AM Paris time, moved in and crawled into bed. Life was good for awhile. Unfortunately, at least according to his wife but unsubstantiated by objective evidence, she woke up some four hours later thinking a train was passing through the heart of their apartment only to find that it was her beloved husband who, according to her, was deep asleep, pretending to be a train. So she got him up and, woozy but alive, they went exploring.

The next three days were blissful. The weather in Paris for November was unseasonably warm and sunny and they spent their time sight seeing, walking and walking and walking, seeing the Louvre and the Musee d'Orsay, and eating and drinking well. They had brought Canadian T shirts and lapel pins just in case, but the conflict over past wars and Freedom Fries versus French Fries was long gone. It turned out the French like nice Americans and for Alex and Will, the reverse was equally true. Mornings were spent drinking American coffee at a small Jewish bakery and coffee shop on Rue du Temple, a block from the apartment.

The fourth morning they got there at their usual time, right around 9:00, found one of the outside tables empty, ordered the pastries to die for and the coffees, and settled in to watch the world of Paris go by. There is a comfort to knowing someone so well that words don't mean a lot when you're in a place that just being there is all there is to know. And so it was that morning for Will and Alex. More time in Paris, a day trip to Versailles on the morrow and two days after that, on to the bike trip.

Life was good. And then very suddenly it wasn't.

CHAPTER THIRTY SIX
CHAOS

For the rest of his life, he would never know why he did what he did in the next seconds of time. Maybe it was partly the instincts of an athlete's life from years ago, maybe it was the roar of the crotch rocket motorcycle as it accelerated down the street, maybe it was the rider dressed all in black looking towards the restaurant. Or maybe it was all those things that, together, focused Will on the machine bearing down on them. And then for sure it was Will seeing the gun pulled from under the black coat and aimed at the restaurant. And at Will and Alex. Time for just a split second froze and then Will moved just as he heard the first shots.

He dove to the right and tackled Alex driving her to the ground. He heard many, many shots and felt a burn across his back as he lay on Alex. There were more gunshots and then an explosion just farther away from them. Exploding glass was everywhere. The sound of the motorcycle faded replaced by sounds of screaming and moaning.

Will lay on his wife for what seemed liked forever but may have been thirty seconds. Sirens now getting closer.

"You OK?"

"You're laying on me, I can barely breathe. Is it over?"

"I think so." He thought he sounded very brave and strong but, sadly, his voice squeaked very badly. He was scared to death. Will was aware of the back of his shirt feeling wet. He rolled off Alex and sat up, Alex following suit. She put her arm around him, felt the wetness and pulled back with blood now on her hand and jacket. Never one to panic, she calmly announced to her husband that he had been hurt. About to give it a closer look, two paramedics appeared suddenly at their sides. They spoke only French which Alex didn't understand but they made it clear they wanted room to work on Will. She scooted over to give them enough room and looked around at the scene of destruction. Police and paramedics were everywhere, the police cordoning off the sidewalk and restaurant and the paramedics working on several people in addition to Will.

For Alex, it was an unspeakable scene from the pleasure of a quiet moment in time with her husband to the chaos of bullets and screaming and more screaming. As she slowly grasped what had happened, she focused on the two medics working on Will. They had been joined by a third woman who, in English, asked if she was all right. What do you say to that, she wondered. Oh sure, couldn't be better. Sitting here amidst broken glass from the windows behind her, wounded or dying people around her, her husband's blood on her clothes. Yes ma'am, couldn't be better. Almost as though she could read her thoughts, the woman introduced herself as Dr. Francone and told Alex that it appeared that Will had suffered one or two superficial wounds to his back and that they were transporting him to the hospital in an ambulance. As she spoke, the other two medics were helping Will to his feet to get on the waiting gurney. Alex had the good sense to check to make sure she had her bag and passport, and grabbed Will's hand as they laid him on his side on the stretcher.

"Just a flesh wound, darlin'," she whispered as she walked next to him. He smiled back at her. "Why did I know that was exactly what you were going to say?"

She followed into the back of the ambulance and took one last look back at the scene. Police tape around the whole area, three or four people being attended to by medics, and two shapes on the ground covered with blankets. The ambulance found a gap in the dozens of police cars and ambulances and raced away, siren blasting.

In minutes, they were at the entrance of an emergency room met by several white coated health care providers. Will was rushed through the doors, past a large waiting room, and through another set of doors. Jesus, Alex thought to herself, it's a damned flesh wound, lighten up. She was approached by a woman who introduced herself in English as a triage nurse. She asked Alex some preliminary questions about where they were staying, how she was feeling, whether she needed anything or wanted some water, and then asked her to sit in the waiting room for a few minutes. Funny how ERs are different here. In Albuquerque, she would have had to have her insurance information first and foremost or agree in blood to sign over her first born before anybody would even look at Will. In Paris, they actually seemed to care about the two of them.

In less than ten minutes, the nurse came to get her and escorted her into the examining room where Will, shirtless, was being bandaged up. The doctor working on him spoke only French but an attendant in the room was explaining to Will that the doctor had put a couple of stitches in the deepest part of the wound but that the rest of it should scab over and heal without incident. He was to return the next day for a dressing change because there would be some residual bleeding and oozing. She told him that he was "very lucky", a phrase Alex found exceedingly odd. If they had truly been 'very lucky', they wouldn't have been anywhere near the goddamn restaurant in the first place.

Once the doctor had finished his work and Will was fitted for a pair of scrub tops to replace his ruined shirt, he and Alex were escorted to another part of the hospital and into a large conference room. Standing at one end of a large conference room were four men, two in police uniforms, two in dark suits. Judge Kennedy had been around cops long enough to know these were the gendarme.

One of the suits spoke passable English introducing himself and the others. He was Chief Inspector Devereaux, next to him was Deputy Chief Inspector Killy, and the two uniforms were Sergeants Guillaume and LeGarde. Bennett, clearly feeling the effects of the pain medication, had a flash back to the old Pink Panther movies and Inspector Clouseau but bit his tongue to keep the giggles in check. Devereaux was clearly in charge and very solicitous of the American tourists who had been caught in the gunfire inquiring about their states of mind, Will's injuries, and tsk tsking the awful coincidence that had taken them to the coffee shop just as the attack went on.

They were told that three people had been killed and seven others, Will included, injured. The motorcyclist/gunman had escaped for now but was the subject of a manhunt in Paris like no other. Will and Alex were assured an arrest was just around the corner. Kennedy had heard that plenty of times in her tenure on the bench back in Albuquerque and idly thought of a needle in a haystack, one motorcyclist in all of Paris where motorcycles and mopeds ruled the world. But it was not her problem. They were safe. No groups had claimed responsibility for the attack but the working model was that it was a part of a wave of anti-Semitism sweeping all of France. There had been other isolated incidents though none so bold as a murderous daylight attack.

Deputy Chief Inspector took over in less than perfect English and asked both Bennett and Kennedy to recount what they remembered. Will remembered more because he had first heard the rising whine of the motorcycle and had seen it approach with the gunman raising his right hand with the weapon. Kennedy had been oblivious until the first shots and Will's flying tackle that pushed her to the ground.

"Did you notice any pattern to the shots?" Killy asked.

"Like what?" Will asked.

"Like was it the same steady sound of shots or was there a change as the motorcyclist went by?"

Bennett thought that was about the most inane question anybody had ever asked. There he was lying on the ground at a French café having barely escaped with his life, his beloved feeling as though she had been run over by a semi, and the Deputy Chief Inspector wondering about the pattern of shots fired. The Pink Panther all over again.

"I really don't remember anything like that at all, Chief. Why are you asking?"

"Oh, just following up on something. Bullet pattern showed several bullets fired in a random fashion, then a long concentrated burst, and then tailing off again, then the explosion. Tailing off at the end maybe because he was reaching for the bomb but the beginning and the middle seem odd to us."

She almost didn't ask the question and in the months to come wished to hell she hadn't but she did.

"Where was the concentration the greatest?"

"Actually, right where you were sitting, Madame. Most bullets, most casualties."

She felt a shiver down her back. She remembered all the tables were full in an outdoor area that spanned maybe 35 to 40 feet and asked why the burst in the middle.

"Madame, we don't know if there is any significance at all. We're checking the identities of the killed and injured to see if there was anything about them that might make them a target but, absent that, probably nothing at all. For now, we think it was a terrorist attack on a Jewish business."

A few more questions and the interview was about to wrap up again with solicitous apologies from the French police. Bennett remembered the bike trip in the south of France that was to begin the next afternoon and was pretty sure he wasn't going to be in any condition to go on it. Wounds may be superficial but rarely so for the person who has been shot. He asked whether the police could help in cancelling their trip and, more importantly, from Will's perspective, getting their money back. The Chief Inspector was almost relieved he could in part restore the Americans' faith in the French. Gathering the details from Alex on the name of the tour, Devereaux said,

"Monsieur, consider it our privilege to be of service and consider it done. We have a car waiting to take you back to your apartment. Sergeant LaGarde?" They each shook hands with the police and followed LaGarde to the front of the hospital. A police car delivered them safely to their apartment, they walked in, and Bennett found the brandy and poured both of them a shot. Then they went to bed and slept the rest of the afternoon away.

Life's a journey.

He woke screaming into his pillow, images of bodies and blood everywhere. Will Bennett didn't know where he was, what time it was, only that the images of carnage seared him and left him sweaty and scared. Alex rushed into the bedroom just as Will began to regain some sanity.

"Shoulder hurts, back hurts," a mumble from the bed.

"Pain meds coming up. What?"

"Blood, bodies everywhere, man on a motorcycle aiming at us. Paris, City of Lights, not supposed to be like this. Jesus, Alex."

"Pain meds coming up, Will. Hang on," She turned to the living room.

"You OK?" he yelled after her.

"Better than you, cowboy, better than you." She thought for a second. But not by much. She too had been startled awake an hour before in part because of nightmares and in part because of the phone. It had been Liz who was up early, had gotten the CNN Headline News about the attack and was checking up, never thinking in a million years, Will and Alex were involved. Kennedy took the high road, assured Liz all was well, and hung up without telling her how close it had been for a couple of Americans in Paris. With a little luck, nobody back in Albuquerque would need to know it was Will and Alex.

No such luck. Within the hour Jackie LaPointe and Liz called from a firm conference room, Liz a little put out that Alex had not been forthcoming now that Albuquerque TV stations were carrying the news that the Honorable Alexandra Kennedy and well known lawyer Will Bennett had narrowly escaped a terrorist attack. Alex downplayed the whole thing telling Liz and Jackie and probably others in the conference room that all was well and that she hadn't wanted to alarm anyone when she had spoken with Liz the first time.

And that wasn't the smartest thing to do with Liz or Jackie, both of whom were extremely protective of Will.

Liz. "They said Will's been shot, Judge." Clipped, angry.

"He's right here. Liz, let me get him."

Will walked out of the kitchen having just popped the French version of a Vicodin and halfway through a glass of Beefeater's Gin. So he might have sounded a little slurred.

"I'm fine, Liz, Jackie. Everything is cool. Life is good." He handed the phone back to Alex. Great, she thought, way to buckle down.

Somewhat mollified that he was at least alive, Albuquerque signed off with Liz waiting for instructions on when she should get them home. Alex told her she'd be in touch. Not a perfect sign off but good enough.

She put the phone down. "If anything ever happens to you, I'm a dead woman, you know that, don't you?"

Vicodin and gin beginning to kick in, Will could only nod his head. "She's always had my back and me hers. Plant the evidence in her house before you do me in."

Alex plunked Will on the couch with American CNN on and went down to the corner store to get enough for a light dinner. He watched with the only half of his brain still working but perked up when the announcer talked of the attack at the Jewish café and the possibility that a Jewish diplomat, in Paris for talks with the French government, may have been the target. He went on to say that the diplomat had been unhurt, that the attacker remained on the loose, and that no group had claimed responsibility which, to this announcer, seemed a bit odd. Will was slightly put off that neither he nor Judge Kennedy got any recognition at all. He drifted.

The judge appeared with two bags of goodies and began to spread them out on the table. Will was half in the bag with his ginvicodin cocktail on board but still reasonably lucid as they spent some time talking about what to do next. Stay in Paris, get home, or split the difference and go home in a week rather than two. They opted for the latter with Will pronouncing that NO TERRORIST WILL DRIVE ME OUT OF THE CITY OF LOVE!!!! She couldn't wait for the Vicodin prescription to run out.

Since that morning with the police, Alex had been chewing on something so off the wall that, given her husband's mental acuity at the moment, she chose not to pursue. But the thought remained. Why the burst of gunfire aimed at exactly where they were sitting. Coincidence or were they the target? In Paris? At a sidewalk café? Impossible but it was still there.

He had some more gin and one more Vicodin, she had some Irish whiskey, and they were in bed by eight. As one might expect he reprised his train imitation. Alex was up most of the night unable to put the uneasiness to rest.

CHAPTER THIRTY NINE
PARIS ADIEU

The next morning came early for both of them. Will much better after hours of drug induced, gin induced stupor, his wife gritty but game. 6:00 AM and off to find a diner. They read the New York Times about the attack, still no group claimed responsibility and still no arrests. A couple of sentences about the New Mexico couple caught in the middle but nothing else. Alex thought that was fine and Will, still just a tad off balance, wishing they'd at least put in their pictures.

Colder this morning with November finally in the air. They still had much on their list of things to do, the police had confirmed the bike trip was squared away, and so they talked about the days ahead. It was Will who finally said, "Alex, I think I want to go home, maybe to Michigan, maybe in time for Thanksgiving. I don't for the life of me know why but I don't feel good here."

Intuition is something Alex Kennedy had always had and she trusted it much like she trusted the Tarot cards. She heard him say the words "I don't feel good here" and something connected deep in her. "You're right, Will, let's go to Michigan. I'll even watch the Lions", a lie both of them knew as soon as she said it.

"Should I call Liz?"

"Too early. Let's call the Chief Inspector."

He had gotten them on a noon flight out of Charles DeGaulle into Detroit Metro at 2:30 PM, business class courtesy of the French Government that both of them pretty much slept through hand in hand shoulder to shoulder, and a short hop to Grand Rapids. They rented a car, stopped long enough to get groceries and a turkey, and got to the lake house just after dark. Fire in the wood stove, a beautiful starry night, and way past their bed time. This time Alex was the train and Will didn't mind a bit.

They were home.

Weather in Michigan at Thanksgiving is a crap shoot with the house odds against you. Most often it's cold and grey, the leaves are off the trees and the specter of winter is in the air. Or it can be like two years before when Will and Alex found Will's best friend dead at the Lake House just ahead of a major blizzard. This Thanksgiving morning they awoke to bright sunshine, windless, and the temperature already in the high 30s.

First order of business was the sage, sausage and bread stuffing into the bird and the bird into the oven. As always, they had overbought on turkey pounds but it was the leftovers that were every bit as good as T day and they weren't going home until the following Monday. Turkey Tetrazinni, turkey soup, turkey sandwiches, cold turkey with hot gravy, it was all good.

Will insisted on a walk on the beach that the New Mexico cowgirl initially balked at and then relented knowing how much the lake and the beach meant to Will. And to her, truth be told. They walked and walked warmed by the sun now far to the south, held hands like the old days, spoke of where they'd been, where they were and where they were going. It had been a journey for each of them long before they had met and, God knows, their time together had at least not been boring. Not always happy, not always good times, but never boring. And on balance a hell of a ride.

The present? Still a hell of a ride but one now clouded with all that the spring and summer had brought them. And Paris. And the uncertainty of what was to come when they got back.

"Should we hang it up, Alex? Put ourselves out to pasture?"

She thought about it for something less than a nanosecond.

"We'd kill each other."

Thoughts of a quiet life together holding hands watching the sun set on themselves disappeared into the quiet lake without a trace. She was right of course. Not necessarily that they would kill each other but both of them knew themselves and each other well enough to know that a quiet life in a retirement community was not ever going to be their cup of tea. Not for a long time. Will didn't think they'd kill each other as much as they might go on a Bonnie and Clyde crime spree that might take out an entire old folk's community. A story that would clearly not end well for sure. Plus there was a full life for both of them even if Will quit trying cases. Alex on the bench for the foreseeable future, both of them teaching, Alex writing a case file for the University of New Mexico Law School. Too much gas left in the tank for the both of them. Plus they had friends in New Mexico who had quit early and, from Will and Alex's perspective, had simply shrunk into small worlds of golf and bridge and martinis at lunch at the club that got them to bed for the night about 6:00 PM. No longer citizens of the world but now in the process of beginning to circle the drain long before their time.

For a moment, Will imagined himself sitting around the card table at the club (of course he would have to join one) playing cards with a bunch of Republicans, all of them on a second or third drink just about ready to totter to the buffet for lunch. She's right, of course, suicide would be a better option. Plus if his partners would quit dying, the future of the firm looked bright with work in the tank and hopefully more to come. If his partners would quit dying.

They were on the last stretch home to baste the turkey, maybe watch the Macy's Parade, maybe gear up for a little bed time when Will, out of the blue, turned to Alex.

"Do you ever think about that French cop telling us the bullet distribution was most concentrated right where we were sitting?"

When Alex was trying plaintiffs' cases, she was known throughout New Mexico for what the opposition called her "game face". Devoid of all emotion, inscrutable, and impossible to read. Will knew it well, especially in their early not so boring years. Only after years did he figure out that her eyes, if you really looked at them and what she was doing with her hands were clues to what was behind the mask.

Will looked at her after he said it, saw the game face, saw her eyes look to the dunes on her right and noticed she stuck her hands in the pockets of her jacket. To the rest of the world, nothing. To Will, an earthquake.

"That would be a 'yes' milady?"

She looked at him and hated that any person, especially a guy, would know her that well.

"Crossed my mind once or twice." Game face.

"Make anything of it?"

"Nope." Game face, eyes still glued on the dunes.

He knew better and was just smart enough to let it be. But if she was thinking what he was thinking, that wasn't good. He saw the smoke from the wood fireplace, picked up the pace a bit, and wondered if she had meant it about the Lions game. Paris would wait.

The parade was on TV and they listened more than watched but it was still fun to see all that was going on. They had been in New York once before over Thanksgiving and thought to go to the parade but by the time they had gotten there, people were six deep along the route so Alex and Will had beaten a hasty retreat to Central Park that was practically deserted and had had a very wonderful day.

Thanksgiving dinner at 1:00 PM and it was all that it could have been. Turkey done to perfection even without that silly little thing that popped up, gravy (Will's specialty) cooked to his mother's specs and without a lump to be found. And with plenty for the leftovers. Mashed potatoes, cranberries, stuffing, a bottle of champagne they decadently drank in the middle of the afternoon, and the Temptations on the CD player as they cleaned up.

It turned out that saying that she would watch the Lions game on Thanksgiving meant she would sit in the same room where the television was for the second half reading a novel on her Kindle and making certain the sound was off for the game. Will took what favors he could gather. What was amazing to him was not that the game was a blow out, which it was and therefore boring even to the announcers, but that it was the Lions who were doing the blowing. When had that happened in recent history?

He knew the second game was too much to ask so he didn't. But it was only 4:00 PM and there were turkey sandwiches on the horizon and there was enough champagne on board that both of them thought a "nap" would be in order.

The sun was already beginning to show signs of moving on to the morrow, the wood stove was cooking, and Will and Alex went to the bedroom and turned in for the "nap."

She would later think that things were heating up pretty well there as well when the phone rang. The phone never rang at the lake house and Alex had thought paying the monthly bill, month after month, year after year, was stupid. Except even with a billion, gajillion towers raping the landscape, there was still no service in the dune where they were. They decided to let it go to voice mail in the interests of what they were trying to accomplish. It didn't help.

The machine kicked in.

"Alex. Will. It's Morton. Glad you guys are OK. Liz gave me this number because she said you came back from Paris early. Can't blame you for that. Listen, something's come up that I was hoping I wouldn't have to bother you with but I need to. Call me." Pause.

"Ellen Phillips has disappeared. Please call me as soon as you get this. 505...714...3520. Again, it's Morton. 505. 714. 3520."

Few things in the world would cause Will and Alex to stop the plane ride before the landing but this was one of them. They caught their respective breaths, laid next to each other, and gathered their thoughts.

Will. Ellen Phillips disappeared. Lunch at the diner, her knee against his. Her long time affair with Ron Johnston. The knock on the door at the Inn and the uncomfortable conversation that led her apparently to Morton Blackwell's room. Joe Hall and the night at the Coppertop. Joe dead in a car wreck. Law firm and the money she brings in. Key Man if she's dead. Disappeared. Shit. What a jumble.

Alex. Shit. I really needed sex. Her husband next to her looking at the ceiling fretting, his wife next to him in heat. She almost laughed to herself. Who switched the testosterone in this family unit?

The phone rang again. This time Alex got up and answered it. After "hello", a pause, and then "yes, Detective." Silence for several minutes and the judge finally said,
"Many thanks for the heads up, Margaret. I think we'll stay here for the weekend unless you need us back before then." Another pause.

"OK then. You've got the number here and here are the cell phones that work if we're not here." Kennedy rattled them off.

"Thank you again, Margaret. Bye."

She walked back into the bedroom and despite herself, liking the drama of the moment as Will waited impatiently for news. She carefully got under the covers, propped the pillows up, and turned to her husband.

CHAPTER FORTY ONE
ELLEN PHILLIPS GONE MISSING

Because of her long history with Judge Kennedy and perhaps because they were both women who had fought long odds along their respective paths, Espinoza had broken a few rules and told Alex more than she probably should have because back in Albuquerque, the disappearance of Ellen Phillips was being handled aggressively as a very active police investigation. It probably also didn't hurt that Will and Alex had been in Paris before Phillips was reported missing.

Ellen Phillips had told the office manager that she was going to take a few days off week before last but would be back in the office after a long weekend. Except that she never showed up on Monday. Or Tuesday. Or Wednesday. Finally, Wednesday afternoon, the office manager, Jamee Dawe, went into Morton Blackwell's office and told him she was worried that nobody had heard from Ellen. They had tried her land line and cell phone and both went to voice mail. Reluctantly, but knowing it was the only thing he could do, he called Detective Espinoza.

Given all that had gone on with the law firm of Johnston & Blackwell PA, Espinoza jumped on the news. By late in the work day, she had gotten a search warrant for Phillips' condo and had led the team that went there. The short version from Espinoza to Kennedy was that it appeared as though Ellen Phillips had indeed decided to leave town for a few days. There was evidence from markings on the bed that she had packed a suitcase, the thermostat had been turned down to a comfortable 60 degrees, the refrigerator had been cleaned out of perishables, and her purse, wallet and ID were gone. Except her car keys were on the counter and her car was in the garage and that was a mystery to the police.

They checked airports, the bus terminal, and the train station and no Ellen Phillips had been seen. The next day they went to her bank and got the unhappy news that a week before, Phillips had closed a savings account with almost $97,000 in it. She had taken it in cash and gave the explanation to the bank officer that she was investing in some land west of Albuquerque. All was in order and the bank sadly closed the account and turned over the money.

For the next several days in the run up to Thanksgiving, there was a flurry of activity with the police interviewing once again members of the firm, friends, colleagues and clients. But other than the message to Jamee Dawe that she was leaving for a long weekend, nobody knew anything.

Ellen Philllips had disappeared without a trace.

Alex paused at the end of her narrative.

"I wanna call Robert." It was almost a blurt from Will. Alex's initial reaction? Oh shit.

Will got out of bed, found his robe, and called Robert in Virginia. The kids had been with their mom and her partner for Thanksgiving and Robert had spent the whole day by himself watching football. Will thought to himself that only guys can understand how nice that is. Alicia had had a family get together so the timing was right. He looked over at Alex. Speaker phone? he mouthed. She shook her head.

Unbeknownst to Alex (thankfully) the two men had kept in touch via email since Robert and Alicia had been in Michigan, although the detective had not heard that it had been Will and Alex who had been in the Paris attack. So that was news to him. As was Ellen Phillips' disappearance. Robert listened without interruption, and Will remembered when the two of them had met two years ago how disconcerting that can be and how it invites the other person to keep talking and talking. The difference between Robert and most other people who did that was that Robert really listened, which is exactly why he was so good at what he did.

Finally, Will's narrative that parroted Alex's was over.

Robert asked the usual questions about trains, planes and bus stations, all of which he knew the police had already figured out.

"Doesn't take a rocket surgeon to figure out there's no such thing as coincidence and this clearly isn't coincidence." Davison paused. "Are the cops thinking that Johnston and Baker are still suicide and accident?"

"She didn't say."

"How could she not?"

"Will, any idea where Phillips got that kind of money on hand in a savings account?"

"Not really. She commanded a pretty hefty hourly rate given what she did, especially by Albuquerque standards, did pretty well by us because of it, and plus we had distributed a chunk of Baker's Key Man life that came in in October. So maybe a combination."

Another pause. "Just thinking out loud but to have that kind of cash on hand could sure lead somebody to thinking there was a plan in place to disappear for some time. I'm just saying."

Will thought about that statement for a few seconds but before he could say anything, Robert had another thought.

"Let's say for argument's sake that Ellen Phillips had a hard on for Ron Johnston because they'd been together for awhile and he'd broken it off for Beverly Davis. She stages Johnston's suicide, then kills Davis because she fucked up her relationship with Johnston. Next, she hooks up with Baker who turns out to be a cretin and she stages that accident leaving enough at the scene and at his office to lead everybody to the conclusion that Baker was a sot and drove drunk off a cliff. Then she gathers enough money that gets her a new identity and a new location and disappears."

Will felt that familiar gastro reflux that he got sometimes under stress and wondered if there were Tums in the bathroom.

"I don't know, Robert. That seems so out of character for Ellen Phillips that she would plan and kill three people just because of bad relationships. She'd told me that her life had been a series of them." And even as the words came out of his mouth, Will's GERD got worse.

"Will." Robert's voice so quiet Will could barely hear it. "Any reason for you to think that she's disappeared because she's looking for you?"

Will's initial reaction was to check the sliders out to the lake to see if anybody was there. This was an isolated place and it was not the first time a psychopathic killer had taken advantage of that. There was nothing to see as darkness had all but fallen, but for good measure Will turned the floods on front and back. He went back to the night at the Inn at Cloudcroft and got a little queasy. Then wondered if he should call Blackwell and share Robert's question with him.

"But if she were doing all of that while she was still with the firm, why disappear if the job isn't done? She knows I'm coming back." Will thought that to be a first rate deflection technique but, of course, for Robert Davison, deflection techniques had been a part of his career from day one.

"It's a good point, Will, but that doesn't mean there is nothing to worry about," Robert having made some connection between Ellen Phillips and Will Bennett.

"Lemme think about it, Robert."

"Fair enough, but if you're concerned at all, you might want to talk to Espinoza, OK?"

"Fair enough. Best to Alicia."

"And the same to Judge Kennedy. And Happy Thanksgiving. Maybe the Lions will get to the playoffs, right?"

"Right, Robert. Thanks for everything. 'Bye." Will hung up the phone.

Alex, who had feigned disinterest throughout the conversation was palpably angry. "What the hell do you mean 'she knows I'm coming back'? What the hell is going on, Will Bennett?"

Uh oh. First and last name, always a bad sign. For a mini-second he thought about doing something less than the Full Monty but knew she would pull it out of him anyways. So he told her what Robert had opined up to and including the concern over Will's well being. He told her about Ellen Phillips ending up with Morton Blackwell that night at the Inn, and then shut up.

She thought for a minute. "You wouldn't think being told 'no' by somebody would make them want to kill you. Hell, you would've been a serial killer long before this if that were true. Plus you're right about disappearing before the job is done. But if I were you, I'd call your partner, Mr. Blackwell. And I'm thinking we ought to get back to Albuquerque sooner than later. Given what we've been through here, I'm getting the creeps. I'll go in the bedroom while you call Morton.

She paused at the doorway. "Robert mention anything else?"

"Nope. Just that he sends his best to you." Will already distracted by getting to the phone. Alex thinking that Robert Davison truly is a stand up guy.

Will dialed Blackwell's cell phone thinking Thanksgiving dinner at the Blackwells ought not to be disturbed by a call to his house. He got voice mail, left the message that Robert had worked on, and told him that he and Alex would get home in the next couple of days. He hung up and hoped to God Davison was wrong.

Will found the bottle of Plymouth's Gin and the two 'up' martini glasses in the freezer left there for the rainy day. He poured them both a martini, put another log in the wood stove, and told Alex the coast was clear.

They spent the first martini talking over Davison's theory and testing it against everything they knew about the deaths of Johnston, Davis and Baker. Means, motive and opportunity were always the three things cops looked at in a murder investigation. Motive was there at least for Joe Baker who had beaten Ellen Phillips and Ron Johnston if she really were that angry. Plus if Beverly Davis were the other woman and Phillips was that hateful, then maybe. Means and opportunity were harder to imagine. They supposed she knew Johnston worked early on Saturdays and figured either to surprise him there or maybe she called him for old times' sake. There might have been time on either side of killing him and staging the suicide to get out to the Heights, convince Beverly Davis to let her in and kill her as well, but it was an almost unimaginable stretch to think it through. By the same token, once you got past that, Joe Baker's death was almost a given especially after what he'd done to her.

Alex got up to make a second martini and the turkey sandwiches and the phone rang. She motioned to Will who picked it up, said "Hey, Morton," and walked into the bedroom.

Five minutes later, the door opened and a martini glass appeared at the end of a long arm and hand. He took it gratefully and returned to the telephone. The door closed softly behind him.

Fifteen minutes later, he emerged from the bedroom with an almost empty glass and the telephone.

"Didn't go that well," he said to Alex. "Pretty much scared poor Morton half to death. Told me it had been a one night stand by agreement, no further discussions, no further trysts, nothing but business as usual. End of story.”

"Then if it's all the truth according to Robert Davison, he shouldn't have anything to worry about. And neither should you.” Sometimes she just couldn't help herself.

CHAPTER FORTY TWO
BACK HOME IN THE DESERT

Will and Alex got back to Albuquerque the Saturday after Thanksgiving. They had spent the better part of Friday cleaning up and driving in for dinner with old friends in Grand Rapids where Will had practiced for so many years before moving to the desert.

He had a long conversation with his daughter, Grace, now in her third year in law school and still wondering if she would ever find a job after graduation. She was in Colorado skiing with the same boyfriend she had now had for two years but promised some days in Albuquerque over the Christmas break after finals were over. He wondered idly about taking time skiing ahead of final exams in your last year of law school, but had learned much from living with Alex on what battles to fight and when to fight them.

One thing about Thanksgiving weekends is that on Wednesday and Sunday travel is impossible. Saturdays are a breeze and they got home in time to get groceries and to pick Hijinks up from the kennel. That much time gone and it clearly would cost the two of them plenty as Jinks was not above resentment and punishment by guilt. Although even she had to admit, it was good to see the two of them. Barely.

Sunday morning, he met with Luis and Morton at the office to talk about what to do with the latest loss to the firm. Sadly and fortunately at the same time, they all knew the drill and they would sit down first thing Monday morning, put together the list of clients, and then refer them to other practitioners in the Albuquerque area. Nobody had anything knew to add other than what Will already knew about the missing Ms. Phillips. The police had gone through her office, taken her computer, but apparently had learned nothing. Still not a word from her. Neither Morton nor Will mentioned the Davison theory to Luis.

After his two partners left, on a whim Will called Jackie LaPointe. She answered on about the fourth ring and it was clear that the call was a wake up call. Will vaguely wondered if she was alone. He asked about life since they'd been gone, assured her he was fine, and then asked about Ellen Phillips. Jackie, like all the others, had given a statement to the police but had nothing to add to what he knew. She did echo Robert's possible theory and the conversation ended with her saying: "Will, you're OK, aren't you?"

And before he could ask what she meant, she hung up.

He called Liz next. She was up and around and clearly not alone and Will thought that was terrific. He held his breath and asked about the "clothes optional" vacation, and Liz assured him that it had been phenomenal but that she would keep the pictures PG rated. They got around to Ellen Phillips and he got the same version only this time, she ended with: "Will, are you going to be OK?"

Clearly the consensus among people closest to him was that there was a madwoman on the loose and Will had a target on his shirt.

What was it that old woman told him one time? Reputations are like your virginity. Once you lose either one of them, they are really difficult to get back. After all the years with Alex, Will's reputation, in some peoples' eyes, led them to believe he was in harm's way.

This time I didn't do anything, he muttered to himself. Why me now?

CHAPTER FORTY THREE
MARGARET ESPINOZA REDUX

Will got home a little after 1:00 PM to find an unmarked police car in the driveway. Not a good sign, he thought to himself, as he let himself in. Alex announced "they" were out on the patio and he went out to find his spouse and Albuquerque Police Detective Margaret Espinoza having iced tea. How special.

Espinoza rose to shake Will's hand and he was reminded of the firmness of her handshake and how strikingly beautiful she was. He also reminded himself that she was a cop who, not so long ago, had had him on a short list of suspects. The only things that had changed had been almost getting killed in Paris and Ellen Phillips disappearing.

To the point. "As I was telling the judge, we are reopening all of the investigations since last April. With Phillips' disappearance there is just too much here to ignore. We may be completely off base but the pattern of relationships that Phillips had been involved in and the way they ended is eerie. I'm here to see if there is anything you can add to the mix."

Will thought all detectives across the country must think the same way and then caught himself. If Jackie LaPointe had figured it out, maybe he was the only one who hadn't. He had the uncomfortable feeling that Alex was measuring him from across the patio.

"Oh, I forgot to mention. Morton Blackwell called me yesterday and we talked about the Inn at Cloudcroft. As of this afternoon, we have him under police protection."

Jeez, Morton. Thanks for the heads up this morning were the words that appeared in the balloon over Will's head.

"We're wondering if we should do the same thing for you and Luis?"

At least she included Luis. That helped a little bit.

Bennett turned to Alex. "What do you think?"

"Maybe for a few days until the police find her. Can't hurt, and if she's this insane, then nobody knows what she'll do."

Espinoza didn't even wait for Will to agree.

"Fine. Consider it done. To be safe, we'll have protection for you here and for both of you at work. In the meantime, we're continuing to do everything we can to track her down, but she truly has fallen off the world. With the cash she has on hand, she can run…or hide…for a long time before she needs to surface. I think this protection is probably unnecessary because we don't think she'd stay here. Too many people know her and could recognize her. Still."

Some pleasantries and the detective was gone. A few minutes later, Will looked out the window and a different unmarked ABQ police car was across the way.

"This is a nightmare, Will. Just a nightmare."

The rest of the day was spent in near silence between the two of them, both going over the past months in their own minds, both frightened in their own ways, both wondering about the future.   Will lost himself in pro football which didn't help the marital situation. Alex found a dog eared copy of *To Kill a Mockingbird* and retreated to the den.

An early dinner, more football, more *Mockingbird* and early to bed for both of them. Sometimes as much as two people can love one another, being apart is the only way to get through the day. Then when you're ready, you come back together which is exactly what happened as soon as they turned out the light. Once the physical coming together was over, the two of them talked about the minute details from that first call last April when they were in Garcia's to now, trying hard not to spare any details and now seeing it through the prism of Ellen Phillips disappearing. Most of it fit. Some of it didn't, but most of it did.

"I hope they find her soon," Will said.

"Me too."

Will Bennett rolled over and went to sleep.

Alex laid awake longer staring out the window at the stars in a beautiful high desert winter's night. There's something not quite right but I can't figure out what, and it's making me crazy. Maybe tomorrow.

The next morning, Will was first to the office followed shortly by Morton, the two of them always the first to arrive and the first of whom was on coffee duty. They were joined by a plain clothes ABQ police officer who accepted a cup of coffee and settled into a chair in the reception area. They had debated where she should position herself and decided up front was best. A second officer was in a car in the alley behind the building.

At 8:30 everybody gathered in the kitchen area. In addition to himself, Luis Moreno and Morton Blackwell were there; Jackie LaPointe; Liz LaRue; Debra Ramirez, Ellen Phillips' assistant; Rebecca Jackson, Luis Moreno's assistant; Ginny Michaels, Morton Blackwell's assistant; and Jamee Dawe. All had noticed the presence of the woman in the severe dark suit in the reception area and Morton started the meeting by explaining her presence. Debra Ramirez stared straight ahead through red rimmed eyes, knowing the officer was there to protect them from someone she thought she knew so well.

Morton spent some time thanking everyone for having stuck with the firm through the last months and remembering the tragedies that had tarnished what had been the brightest of hopes for the future. He remembered each of the people who they had lost, asked them to pray for Ellen Phillips (although Will thought that a little over the top), and then talked about moving on.

Monday would be spent with Debra Ramirez and Morton Blackwell going over Ellen's client list and open matters and contacting each of the clients with a list of referral attorneys, a list that Morton had spent most of Sunday afternoon compiling and making contacts at home with the lawyers. The rest of the firm would go back to work. There was still plenty of that to be done and one of the few advantages to this law firm was that each lawyer worked for the most part independently of the others. Phillips' clients needed to be taken care of, but other than the loss of production that she personally brought to the firm, it would be all right financially.

Will wondered about the Key Man on Ellen. Do you get it if you can't find her and somehow she had killed the others? Or do we get Ron Johnston's if they prove she killed him? Jesus, Will, you are pathetic, he said to himself. Across the room, he saw Jackie looking at him and wondered if she were reading his mind. Yuck.

Morton opened the meeting for questions or for anybody to say anything. This collection of individuals all from different backgrounds and different histories thrown together and sticking together through it all. So far. It was Jamee Dawe again this time who spoke up and talked about exactly that, that they all had each other and somehow that made what they were going through a little bit better. Jackie asked whether the rumors about Ellen Phillips being sighted both in Albuquerque and as far away as Denver and San Francisco had any merit, and nobody knew the answer to that one either.

Finally, by 9:30 nobody else had anything to say and the firm went to work.

Bennett spent the rest of the morning trying to catch up with what had accumulated on his desk since he had been gone. As she always had, Liz had separated it into piles of Need to See Now, Need to See Soon, and See If You Want To. Will always started with that latter pile because it made him feel better to make his desk cleaner sooner.

He was almost through the Need to See Now pile when noon arrived and, by agreement, Morton, Luis and Will went to the Coppertop to talk about the future of Johnston & Blackwell. They settled in the corner booth, ordered up ice teas and green chile cheeseburgers all around, and then got to it. Morton's plate was more than full and thought he could keep a young lawyer, especially one with a book of business, busy full time. Luis and Will had a lot of cases in the pipe line as well, but because it was contingency work, it was a different breed of cat. There were paydays only when a case settled or they won it and thousands of dollars in costs to be fronted in the meantime. Both Will and Luis were certain they had a good stable of cases most of which would pay out in the long run. The question was whether the hourly work of Morton Blackwell could keep the firm afloat until that happened. What helped was that the firm had been very conservative in dealing with the Munson medical malpractice fee as well as the Baker Key Man. There was money in the bank and the line of credit was down to zero.

Both Luis and Will thought they could use another young lawyer who didn't need to have a book of business and Bennett wondered to himself whether Grace Bennett would ever be interested in moving to Albuquerque. They talked about other laterals they might approach, but wondered if anybody would really want to join a firm that seemed as snake bit as Johnston & Blackwell.

Business and lunch over about the same time, the three of them looked at each other with the single question hanging in the wind. Does it make sense for the three of us to stay together? With his family and political connections, Morton could go anywhere…to another firm or start his own all over again. Luis' reputation in the community assured him of the same thing. Of the three, Will was the most vulnerable because he had taken the biggest risk…leaving a well established defense firm to strike out on his own. How many of the plaintiffs' cases they had in the office would stay with a Michigan transplant was, at best, problematic.

It was Luis who answered the question first. "I like what we have, gentlemen, and what we've been through only makes me more convinced that I did the right thing coming over here. I'm staying."

Morton was next. "If Luis is staying, I'm staying."

Both of them looked at Will who Luis would later say had tears in his eyes.

"I'm in."

The rest of the day flew by for Will. He checked with the judge half way through the afternoon and told her about the lunch. She was thrilled. He called Liz and Jackie into the office and told them that the firm was solid and moving on and they were thrilled.

Morton called the rest of the people into the break room and announced the same thing. All were thrilled but for Debra Ramirez who somehow felt like the odd one out. Blackwell assured her that there were plans for expansion for the firm and she would be a part of it. That helped them all.

By the end of the day, all piles on Will's desk had been taken care of one way or the other, and in some ways he felt like he'd never left. And given what he and Alex had been through, that was probably the best thing he could say.

He had told Alex he would stop by Monroe's and get dinner, accomplished that task, and arrived home just as the judge did. Monday Night Football had started but he knew Thanksgiving and yesterday were way pushing his luck. He made them both a drink, got the TV tables out, and let Alex pick the old movie on TCM. A perfect night except for the unmarked police car across the street and still nothing new about Ellen Phillips. It was off the front page.

The next morning was extra early. The judge had to get her car in for service, Will had an office day, and he followed her to Community Automotive, picked her up and dropped her off at work.

Judge Kennedy let herself in through the security door and had the luxury of a good hour before the madding crowds arrived. She relished this time alone and the silence of a courthouse that would soon teem with what passed for justice in Albuquerque, New Mexico. Her case manager and best girl friend, Karen Stillson, would be along in an hour or so. She tried again to make sense of it, tried to think of what she was missing, and still couldn't get to it. Something.

Head in hands, elbows on the desk, deep in thought, Judge Alex Kennedy heard a door to her chambers open and close quietly and froze. There was security from the public halls with card access to the judicial chambers, but security was more the exception than the rule. The private security firm hired by the county had said they would look into it. They hadn't. She looked at her watch and it was still only 7:50 AM. Nobody on the county payroll, save a couple of judges like herself got there, before 8:30.

Silently and still without breathing, Kennedy reached for her desk drawer on the right, slowly opened it, and pulled the loaded .38 Caliber handgun from its place. She let out a breath and waited for what was to come. She could hear noises in Karen's office adjoining hers and wondered vaguely if it were robbery. Stupid. Nobody would be so stupid they would break into a courthouse, break into a judicial corridor and then break into a judge's chambers just to rob it. No, this was far different.

The door opened and the judge raised the gun. Will Bennett stood in the doorway.

"Hi honey, forgot your briefcase in my car." He stopped in his tracks noticing that his wife seemed to be aiming a gun at him.

Kennedy let out a whoosh of air. "Jesus H. Christ, Bennett. You fucking trying to get yourself killed? Why don't you knock, for Christ's sake!" The gun went down to the desk still in her hand.

He wondered if he'd had an accident, took a moment to feel if there was any evidence in the form of a wet spot on the front of his pants, and decided he had avoided at least that humiliation. He quietly put the briefcase on the floor inside the judge's office, mumbled an apology and said something about calling him if she needed a ride at the end of the day. He walked out of chambers, got to a drinking fountain, and stood for what seemed like minutes alternately drinking and dunking his face in the tepid water of the Bernalillo County Courthouse. God damn, that was scary. On the way out of the courthouse to his own office, he got to thinking about that headline**: Judge Kills Off Another Johnston & Blackwell Partner (and her husband).** Wonder if Espinoza would have forgotten Ellen Phillips and tried to get the judge for everybody else? Naw, probably not. Just chalk this one up to male stupidity.

Needless to say, the rest of the day had to go better. Alex and Karen had a great laugh out of her almost killing her husband and Will didn't mention it to anybody. He and Luis and Jackie met for most of the early afternoon on a case that was going to trial in the late winter and exhibit heavy. The team needed Jackie to work her magic with the software, a task she reveled in. Somewhere along the line he got a message from Alex that the car wouldn't be ready until tomorrow but that Karen would give her a ride home. Maybe a walk to Seasons for dinner?

He left about 6:00, already dark now that the end of November had arrived, and got home minutes later. No lights on in the house so he let himself in, got some lights on, said hello to Jinks, and heard a knock at the front door. Without a thought, he opened it and faced Jamee Dawe.

They say that in times of crisis, time slows down to a crawl as in 'I saw my whole life passing before me.' What passed through Will's mind were several things. Wow, she is so tall. And so beautiful. And she has a gun in her right hand pointed at me. It's not a big gun but it's pointed at me so that makes it big. In the background, he could hear the faint sounds of sirens but for now all there was was silence.

"May I come in, Will?" She took a step forward and he backed up into the living area. She followed and was maybe four or five steps away from him still holding the gun aimed at his midsection.

An octave or two lower than it should have been, Will croaked, "Jamee. Whadda you doing? Put that thing down. Why?" Sirens now louder and louder.

He saw her lips move in what might have passed for a smile. "Will. You are one down and one to go…"

There is something both universal and unmistakable about a shotgun being cocked even for the most naïve of people. At the sound, Jamee turned to her right to the stairs where the sound had come from.

Alex Kennedy was on the second stair from the bottom holding the shotgun at waist height. A powerful blast that echoed in the room caught Dawe full on in the chest and propelled her into the china cabinet some five feet behind where she was standing. The cabinet and china collapsed around and over her.

Bennett was frozen in place. Margaret Espinoza was coming through the front door with gun in hand, two uniforms behind her, two more uniforms were breaking in through the patio door. Kennedy was standing still holding the shotgun in ready position.

Police guns trained on what was left of Jamee Dawe, an officer was feeling for her jugular, and shaking his head. More sirens in the background. Guns put away, the shotgun gently taken from Kennedy, and the police were standing down.

Espinoza. "I am so sorry we didn't get here sooner. We had put it together finally this afternoon, went to arrest her, and she was gone. Figured she was either coming here, going to Blackwell's, or trying to get away. Surveillance never saw her so she must have come in through the neighbor's and around the car port."

Will looked at his wife still standing on the stairs. "What are you doing home?"

CHAPTER FORTY SIX
REQUIEM

It seemed like hours passed while the police, crime scene people and medical examiners all scoured the town house. Will and Alex sat out on the patio and let the pros do their business. Neither said anything because there was nothing to say. They held hands and breathed in the high desert night air. It calmed them both.

Espinoza finally came out and told them that the crews were done but that she thought it might be a good idea for them to get a hotel room for a couple of nights.

Kennedy asked the obvious. "Why?"

"Jamee Dawe and Ellen Phillips were lovers, had been for as long as Jamee had been in Albuquerque. They met soon after she moved here and had had a relationship all that time through all the men Ellen went through. We have much to put together but we think Dawe was keeping score out of jealousy, rage, hatred of men or all of the above."

Will this time. "How did you figure her?"

"One small mistake, really. She was the one who said Ellen was going away for a few days, remember? When I talked with Debra Ramirez, she was surprised that Phillips would not have told her. It was a first. So on a hunch, I asked Ramirez to see Ellen Phillips' estate plan. All of it went to Jamee's daughter. We got a search warrant for Dawe's apartment and Phillips had co-signed for it. Found some notes and love letters that were unsigned but that we were pretty sure were from Ellen Phillips based on the handwriting we had gotten from her office. There was a car loan that was also co-signed by Phillips. When we went back to the bank that had given her the money, we found out that Jamee Dawe had a right of survivorship if something happened to Phillips."

“But Ellen withdrew the money herself.”

“And there is the loose end. Ellen Phillips is missing and Jamee Dawe will never tell us where she is. Good night. Please get a hotel room.”

As she stood up, Alex had a thought. “Paris?”

The detective stopped and looked at her and then at Will. “We think so. She took a few days off herself right in that time frame. I’ll let you know when I know.”

They followed Espinoza back into the town house and said good night at the front door. Closed it and locked it, and they surveyed what was left of the living room, body gone, much of the blood from the chest wound cleaned up, and now just the carnage of what had been all of the mementos and childhood collections of Alexandra Kennedy. Will went into the kitchen to make them a drink and came back out to find Alex sitting in the midst of what was left of the cabinet and her priceless treasures. She was sobbing in a way that he had never seen and it paralyzed him. Awkward for a moment, he handed her the glass of Jameson’s and then sat down beside her amidst the broken pieces of her past. Nothing to say but to be there.

After awhile, the sobbing quieted and she took a sip, her hands bloody from the little cuts of trying to find whole pieces of her past. Will saw something to his left and picked it up. It was the small statute of Rachel that her dad had given her just a year before he died. It was her most treasured and it was whole. As carefully as he could, he passed it over to her. She put her glass down, took it in both hands and held it tightly to her chest. Tears in her eyes, she turned to her husband.

“It’s a start, isn’t it?”

EPILOGUE
LOOSE ENDS

They spent the night at the townhouse after all. Jinks was there, the pieces of crystal were there, and they were there. They watched the news at 10:00 and again at 11:00. There was film of the townhouse, although neither Will nor Alex had ever been aware of the TV trucks, pictures of the two of them taken from file copies, a short press conference in which the Albuquerque Chief of Police announced the details of the events of that night with Detective Margaret Espinoza conspicuously in the background behind the chief. The reporters duly noted that Ellen Phillips was still missing and the search for her was continuing. There was a short bio of Jamee Dawe and word that Protective Services had taken her daughter from Ms. Dawe's apartment and were caring for her pending notification of the next of kin.

Will remembered back to how surprised he was that Jamee had wanted to join a brand new firm given her position with an established prosperous one, and now thought it was that she wanted to be closer to Ellen Phillips. And how she had been the one to say "We are family". The duration and depth of the relationship between the two women would likely never be fully uncovered. Other than the suspicions about the deaths of Ron Johnston, Beverly Davis, and Joe Baker, nothing concrete was ever found and the cases were closed again. The gun that Dawe had the night she tried to kill Will was owned by Ellen Phillips but without finding Phillips, that was also a dead end. Dawe's passport showed she had been in Paris the same day as the terrorist attack on the Jewish café, but the police in France could never connect the dots and the attack remained unsolved. Another dead end.

Ellen Phillips was never found.

Alex Kennedy never did remember what it was that had troubled her so.

The Dawe case was finally closed as a case of assault on Will Bennett and defense of another by Judge Alexandra Kennedy.

For awhile, both Morton Blackwell and Will Bennett continued to have police protection, but after a couple of weeks and budgetary cuts, those were eliminated. It was some weeks before either of them wasn't from time to time looking over their backs.

Johnston & Blackwell PA kept the name of the firm. It hired two new business associates, one a sixth year woman out of one of the larger corporate firms who had her own book of business, one a brand new graduate out of the University of New Mexico. It found a terrific litigator when Kennedy was asked to teach at a Public Services Attorneys' Program in Boulder and a Legal Aid lawyer from Albuquerque knocked her socks off with her poise and grit.

Grace Bennett decided to accept a clerkship for a District Judge back in Grand Rapids after graduation so she could be closer to her mother and friends. Her long time boyfriend had found a job as an associate after graduation with the best known litigation firm in Grand Rapids if not the state. They were going to be living together in the old historic district and now when he brought it up, Grace no longer so easily dismissed the notion of marriage. She came to Albuquerque for a few days over Christmas and had never been happier. Nor had Will.

Over Christmas, Robert Davison and Alicia Young were married in a quiet civil ceremony in Northern Virginia. Will was the best man. For reasons unknown to him, Alex Kennedy begged off going saying there was too much work to do before the end of the year. She was missed.

In late winter and early spring of the next year, Will and Luis tried two plaintiffs' cases back to back with strong verdicts in both. The two of them, along with Blackwell, had become the very best of odd couple friends. Liz was living with her boyfriend and kept looking younger and younger. Jackie LaPointe had taken over as office manager as well as head IT person and had been admitted to law school in the fall at UNM. She was promised a job with Johnston & Blackwell as soon as she graduated. She was dating an anesthesiology resident at UNM Hospitals.

Judge Kennedy had been named Chief Judge of the Second Judicial District Court. She had, as best she could, tried to replace what was lost of the crystal pieces destroyed in the shotgun blast. Rachel was center stage.

In spring, after the second of the two trials, Will and Alex were in the hot tub with a bottle of champagne. Joining them was Hijinks and the newest addition to the family, a black rescue cat, almost a twin look alike of Jinks, they had named Josephine Baker.

Will raised his glass to Alex. "I'm not sure I ever thanked you for saving my life that night. So thank you."

"And I'm not sure I ever thanked you for finding Rachel that night. So thank you." She raised hers to him.

They were silent for a moment and Alex, rubbing Josie's ears to quiet purring, thought to herself that even in the dead ends of so many things, people dying, people moving on, relationships ending or never really starting, there were always the beginnings of some things new.

She would hold on to that for as long as she lived.

9 781936 243433